JUST A BIT OF BANTER, LIKE...

First Published in Great Britain 2013 by Mirador Publishing

First edition: 2013

Any reference to real names and places are purely fictional and are constructs of the author. Any offence the references produce is unintentional and in no way reflects the reality of any locations or people involved.

A copy of this work is available through the British Library.

ISBN : 978-1-909220-55-3

Mirador Publishing
Mirador
Wearne Lane
Langport
Somerset
TA10 9HB

Just A Bit Of Banter Like...

By

Chris Westlake

Mirador Publishing
www.miradorpublishing.com

Prologue

Ogmore-by-Sea, just outside Bridgend, South Wales, summer of 2003

"Well, we're not *really* fishing, are we?" Den asked, inhaling a roll-up in his left hand and slurping a warm beer from his right.

Sam, who had been lying flat on his back, raised his head and looked curiously from side to side, reminding me of a meerkat.

"What do you mean we aren't *really* fishing?" Sam asked. "We have three fishing rods, right? And on the end of the fishing lines are hooks, and attached to those hooks are rag worms, no? I hereby put forward to the learned jury; does this not indicate that some form of fishing is taking place? Now, I'm personally hoping that these rag worms are doing their best sexy wriggle in the water, seducing the weak, hungry fish..." and he lazily shuffled his body about a bit – but only just a bit - as if illustrating what his idea of a worm wriggling sexily looked like, "and you're suggesting to me and Nick here – both of us considered reasonably sane and intelligent members of society – although, admittedly, possibly me more so than Nick – that we are not *really* fishing?"

Fair play, my mate seemed truly exasperated.

"So, Den - let me ask you – if we are not fishing, then what exactly *are* we doing here, in the Goddamn middle of the night, when we could be doing something better – like, I don't know – just sleeping, for example?"

It was a good question, and well delivered, so I thought. It would have earned a mild, polite round of applause on *Question Time*, no doubt. Den, however, seemed unfazed. His casual demeanor changed not one bit. The guy *still* looked barely alive.

"What I mean is, it's not really about the fishing, is it?

The rods, the tackle, the bait – they are all props really, aren't they? It's all about the three of us having some beers and chilling out, spending some quality time together." He paused and took another toke of his roll-up. "I personally have no intention of catching any fish."

Sam went all high-pitched now. "Oh my days," he said. "You are a fisherman who doesn't want to catch any fish? You must be the worst fisherman in the whole of Wales, Den. You're probably worse than most of the English fishermen, too – at least they *try* to catch fish…"

He droned on a bit more, just as Sam tended to do – he was definitely the chatty one of the three - but it was all just banter, really. Sam had shown less intuition and skill as a fisherman than any of us. We'd been at the mouth of the Ogmore River since just before seven o'clock. It was gone twelve now, and there had not even been the slightest indication of a nibble. The fish must be on some latest milkshake fad diet or something. It had been a beautiful summer evening when we'd arrived. My eyes took in everything: the tangled reams of blue and white fishing line washed up on the shore, the brittle kettle fish, flakes of charcoal from a barbecue. The sun was orange and bright and it slowly began fading into nothingness. The spiraling car park was full of vehicles, and couples walked their dogs along the long stretch of sandy beach.

Five hours later, and it was just the three of us, in pitch blackness. The waves in the Bristol Channel rippled peacefully. The sand dunes expanded into the distance. The stars above suggested so many possibilities. On one hand, the world seemed so much bigger out here. On the other, I felt like a tiny dot in a never-ending galaxy.

My thoughts of life and beyond were disturbed by the sound of Den taking a piss. He seemed to do everything loudly, apart from talk. He had a soft, almost appealing voice, if truth be told, though I'd never tell him that. Hot steam rose from an innocent, defenseless rock. He conscientiously diverted his erratic spray so that it splashed against an abandoned shopping trolley. God knows how it got there. The closest supermarket was at least three miles away.

“Just think,” Sam said, “these rocks have probably been here for about forty million years or something, yes? I imagine that young Den here is probably just the latest in a long chain of ancestry to have taken a leak against that very rock. In his own way, he is adding to our history, right there, right now,” he added, thoughtfully.

Den zipped up his fly and returned to his original, dry rock. “Just doing my bit,” he said, with a swagger.

I was feeling unusually reflective tonight. Maybe it was from being at one with nature. More likely, however, it was from the eight cans of lager I’d drunk. I could not help dwelling on the fact that there were eleven days until we went back to school for our final A-Level year. I pictured our school, just a few miles up the road, lying completely silent, occupied only by shadows and darkness, and thought how, in less than two weeks, it would be overrun with pupils and teachers and hopes and possibilities.

The three of us had met in the very first week of comprehensive school. It had been a wet Thursday afternoon, straight after lunch. Half the boys in the first year were huddled together in the hall for our first games lesson. It was the lesson all of us had marked out when we were given our timetable two days before. We sat in white shorts and bare feet on cold wooden benches. The games teacher, Mr Thomas, wore his infamous tight shorts and flannel vest and paced up and down the hall, ready to strike at any moment. His neck tensed, his nostrils flared, his biceps bulged.

“Get into groups of three,” he bellowed, suddenly. “And I mean now, boy!”

Hundreds of eleven-year-old-boys, high on additives and e-numbers, manically scurried around in every direction. I stood up, like everyone else, but everything was such a blur. I could not work out whether to move left, right, forwards or backwards. And so, accepting my fate, I sat down again. The benches began to clear. It felt like children were replaced by a cold, taunting fog. All it needed was a dramatic drum roll and my misery would be complete.

I looked up and expected to be on my own. My nickname was to be Billy. The name would stay with me throughout my painful, lonely school years. I'd talk about it to psychiatrists in distant years and say that it could all have been so different if only I'd stayed on my feet in that cold hall on a wet Thursday afternoon when I was eleven.

Only, none of it was to be. When I looked up, there were two other isolated figures on the benches. One was a skinny, geeky-looking white boy with NHS glasses. The other was a skinny, geeky-looking black boy with NHS glasses. They both eyed me suspiciously, calculating whether they could do better. Reasoning that it was last chance saloon, the white boy shrugged his narrow shoulders, and we linked as a three.

And, I guess we'd been three ever since. Me – Nicholas Evans, and my two best friends, Dennard Jones and Sam Thornton.

"What the fuck?" Sam yelled now. "Nick, your rod is dipping! You've only gone and caught something!"

I looked at my rod, and yes, there was an undeniable dip. Only, I wished that there wasn't. I was comfortable lying there motionless, my hands stuck to the black tar covering the pebbles. I estimated that it was at least eleven feet to my rod, and then, once I'd reached the rod, I'd have to reel the fish in, which was just added effort. And I didn't even *like* fish. Sam and Den were already on their feet, and I felt I had no choice but to follow them.

"It's a big fucker," Den exclaimed as I struggled with the reel. "It's probably a conger eel or a cod, knowing these waters," he continued, suddenly an expert angler.

The weight was not really all that bad, however. I was just feeling weak, tired and drunk. I secretly hoped that the fish would make a miraculous escape and save me from all this pain. It was getting closer. There was an outline. It wasn't a fish at all.

"Oh my days," Sam gasped, open-mouthed. "It's a body!"

It was a sign from the heavens, I thought. This was a crossroads in our lives, and things would really never be the same again.

Den interrupted my thoughts. Taking another toke on his roll-up, he casually slurred, "nah, it's just a bicycle helmet, dipshit." His blurred eyes examined the item closer. "It's not even a very good one, either," he evaluated. "I don't think it's a name brand or anything."

We packed up after that and headed back to our tent, which was on the other side of the river, down by the castle. We crossed the stepping stones. Den counted fifty-one stones, I counted fifty-three, and Sam counted fifty-five. It made me wonder just how pissed we all were. Den was texting on the way back. "Run out of beer," he moaned, as if to his phone.

It seemed to be even darker walking towards the tent. The dim streetlamps were no longer visible. I had not realized just how far in the middle of nowhere we were. I was relieved when we reached the tent, I can tell you.

"Of course, legend has it that ghosts have occupied the old castle for hundreds of years," Sam said, stifling a bored yawn. "I guess it may look like just an old ruin to you and me, but to them, it is still a fortress, and apparently, they guard it fiercely."

"How do you mean?" I asked.

"I don't have any specific details," Sam replied. "And remember, it is all just legend. But, put it this way, some of the disappearances down by the river have conveniently defied rational explanation, if you know what I mean?"

He was winding us up, of course he was, and it was only me who seemed to be taking a blind bit of notice. Den was on his phone again. I thought I could hear something, far away. It sounded like it was coming closer. If silence was unnerving, then sound was absolutely terrifying.

"What's that noise?" I asked.

"Probably just one of the ghosts," Sam replied. "I'm sure that it's nothing to worry about, Nicholas."

"No, serious," I added. "There's something coming towards us."

Silence filled the tent for a just a few deathly moments. I huddled close to Den.

"He's right," Sam said, eventually. His previous, taunting voice was now not so confident.

"Sounds like motorbikes," Den commented.

Of course it was, I realized. The motorbike engines were

revving loudly. Headlamps were cutting through the darkness like City through a Swansea defence. The bikes were making rapid progress. They got closer and closer until they were possibly just hundreds of yards from our tent. The bikes circled us. There must have been five or six of them.

"Hell," Sam exclaimed. "They are going to kill us. We're only seventeen, and I'm still a virgin, for fuck's sake!" he said, wildly slapping his forehead with a hand.

"There are so many things I haven't done in my life," I agreed. My voice was unrecognizable. It was filled with blind panic.

"So you're a virgin too?" Sam asked, hopefully.

"Am I fuck!" I shouted back, offended.

The sound of the engines stopped. The headlamps switched off. Heavy, determined feet walked towards us. There was no denying it now. We were done for.

"So if you had been given the chance, what would you have done with your lives then?" Den asked. It seemed an apt question.

"Just to have been a success," I babbled. "For my mum to have talked about how great I was for a change, and not how wonderful every other fucker is."

"To hell with all that success stuff," Sam bleated excitedly. "All I wanted was to be myself, not what everybody else wants me to be, not my mum, my teachers; nobody. Was that too much to ask?" he shouted, pleading to the heavens.

Our hysteria was interrupted by the unzipping of the tent door. I screamed at the top of my voice. The sleeping bag was pulled over my head and I shut my eyes. I waited to be axed or shot, or possibly both.

Instead, all I could hear were Den's distinctive tones, followed by laughter. "Chill out, ladies, it's just my brother with some more beers," he said.

I pulled my face from inside the sleeping bag. Den's older brother, Patrick, had his face dipped inside the narrow entrance to the tent. He was carrying a crate of Fosters and his big white smile was wider than I'd ever seen it.

"Can't wait to tell your mums about this," was all that Den said.

Chapter One

Moving from Wales to Italy is like moving to a different country – Ian Rush

London, late summer 2011

The world is a wonderful, wonderful place.

It is three o'clock on a standard, no thrills Thursday afternoon, and we are the rowdy suits sat in the corner of the bar.

Not that we can claim to be the only rowdy suits in the corner of this swanky establishment situated smack bang in the City of London at three o'clock on a standard, no thrills Thursday afternoon, for there are replicas of us in every corner. The other tables, the outsiders, are occupied by singletons, identical men in their forties with grey suits and black spectacles, sipping from whiskeys and glancing at the *Financial Times*.

I pull the card out of the machine and catch my reflection in the mirror across the barmaid's shoulder, the one that stretches the full length of the bar. I've gained some extra padding over the years, especially on my cheeks, but there's no denying that Nick Evans is still a lanky git; at 6'2 I still weigh less than twelve stone in my socks. The fine fair hair is parted in a perfect straight line at one side. My moisturised skin is blemish-free. The barmaid catches me winking at myself in the mirror. Her face gives nothing away, which is probably just as well.

I expertly balance the Jaeger bombs on a metallic tray and return to our table. My four drinking partners grab appreciatively at the drinks.

"Thank you, boyo," Bruce says, one eye facing left, the other eye facing right. "Look boyos, boyo has come back with drinks!"

I give the guy a friendly slap on the back. His shirt feels a bit damp. The alcohol probably seeps through his pores. I know the score, though. I'm the Welsh guy of the pack and so I'm a boyo who shags sheep, my Dad is Tom Jones, my Mum is Shirley Bassey, my sister is Charlotte Church, we own a pet dragon and our garden is overflowing with daffodils. It's all good, like.

Its four minutes past three in the afternoon now and the drinks are flowing. The guards are down. The gum shields are off. There is only one way that it is going to go from here, and that's downhill.

"Seriously though, do you speak Welsh, then, Nick?" Lawrence, or it could be Ken, asks me.

I tell him what I tell everyone when I'm asked this question. I feel like a parrot reciting the lines he's memorised. "We don't really speak Welsh much in South Wales," I say. "It's spoken more in north and west Wales, you know? I do know the basics, though," I continue. "I did it for GCSE. That was a long time ago now, though, wow it must be ten years or something. Wish I had done it for A-Level, now. But people told me and my mate, Den, to do something more useful. What was I going to do with Welsh, they asked me, get a job on *Pobl Y Cwm* or *Scorio*? So I did something useful – philosophy. I plan to learn Welsh more, though," I tell them, whoever it is who is asking at the time, "get a book out and teach myself, like. It's difficult though, isn't it, when you are not living in Wales any more, and all that?"

I say the same thing, every time, without fail, and to be honest, it bores me.

It seems a long, long time ago Paul and I arrived at the *Lasocte* offices, but thinking about it, it was only ten o'clock this morning. Paul, his hair slicked back, wearing a new slim-fit Armani suit and a fitted Paul Smith shirt. I was sporting a single-breasted Ralph Lauren suit and a black Pink shirt. Paul gave me a nod and headed to the toilet for his now customary pre-meeting warm-up routine. I imagined him psyching himself up in the mirror. Whatever he does, it always works. He came out of the toilet buzzing and ready for action, a real livewire on a mission. He always starts the talking, confident as you like. I'm happy with that. I'm the right-hand man.

"Gentlemen, you know and I know that we have all met before," he began, with a wry, calculated smile, "but just to conclude formal introductions, I am Paul Richards, Senior Account Manager at *360 Ltd*. And this gentleman to my right is Nicholas Evans, also an established Account Manager at *360 Ltd.* I think I speak both on behalf of myself and Nick when I thank you for accommodating us today. Nick, if you would kindly hand out the proposed agenda…"

This was my cue to do something and, frankly, I was glad, because I was getting bored. I'd heard the spiel hundreds of times before and I was just nodding my head and smiling and oohing and ahhing, exercising both my verbals and my non-verbals, all that stuff we'd covered on that course we did, but really my mind had drifted and I was thinking about what shirt and tie combination to wear tomorrow and whether, because it was a Friday, I should put on my Welsh dragon cufflinks. But now I had the proposed agenda to hand out and so I was on my feet and my mind was momentarily occupied. The three men stared intently at the sheets of paper (quality, crisp white) and for a moment I wondered whether they were genuinely interested in the content, but then I instantly dismissed the thought. Of *course* they weren't interested.

Our job, in a nutshell, is to manage a portfolio of clients, and to ensure that the said clients continue buying our regulated examinations, training courses and study aids; by whatever means is at your disposal. There is no avoiding the Excel spreadsheets and the presentations, detailing all the facts and figures, and then there is all the regular contact by phone and email. But it also means keeping the clients sweet; and how you do so is pretty much up to you. For us two, it means giving them such a crazy time that the client will justify staying with you for a multitude of reasons, but in reality because they just don't want to miss out on any of the fun.

"Gentlemen, we all know that, with the current difficult climate, organisations have needed to make adjustments, and some have them have been difficult and some have been brutal. However, I am sure you will agree that amongst the doom and gloom, hidden away somewhere, there is opportunity. You may need to look hard, and sometimes it may need to be created, but the opportunity is there. Now, only the smartest organisations will locate this opportunity, but I am absolutely adamant…" Paul paused for a moment, leant forward so that his elbows pressed against the table, then twisted his head elaborately from left to right, "…no, I am *certain*, that working closely together, both *360 Ltd* and *Lasocte* can become stronger, more efficient and, ultimately, even more prosperous…"

It was proper, liberating, invigorating text-book stuff that would probably have given our big boss man, Max Vaughan, a semi, but I was still having difficulty concentrating, possibly because I'd heard the same speech last week when we visited *Aratica.* I was thinking about the programme on TV I watched last night about the prejudice 'little people' are subjected to, and I remembered the time Den pulled a short bird in Swansea and I gave him a shed load of abuse. Were my actions honourable, I ask myself, or maybe, possibly, a bit harsh? Mind you, I reminded myself, it was only 'banter' and 'banter' has no limitations…

"…If you are with us, gentlemen," Paul continued, becoming more and more elevated, "I promise you that you are in for one hell of a ride…"

And three hours later, in the bar, not the boardroom, we are still talking about rides.

"Paul says that your woman is a great ride, taffy," Bruce says. Lawrence slams his drink down on the table and whisky spills over the edge of the glass and he bursts into a fit of hysterics and the others join in, eyes watering, legs excitedly crossing and uncrossing.

Our three clients are Bruce, Lawrence and Ken from *Lasocte,* but they might just as well be Dwayne, John and Adam from *Aratica* or Tony, David and Mike from *UCES.* They are just different names, different faces, really.

The ongoing joke is that my girlfriend, Katie, gets around the track more times than Mo Farrah. I don't mind. The thing is, I know that it's a compliment, really. They all fancy her.

See, whichever way you look at it, Katie is a stunner. She is a trophy bird, and that suits me just fine. Katie has been on my arm for six months now, and she is good as gold. *She is well fit mate,* one of them quips (Ken? Lawrence?), *but then I've only seen her from behind.* I've heard it all before. Different people, same jokes.

The drink is starting to give me a warm glow. My face feels like it is melting. We move onto a bar on Lower Thames Street, then another at Tower Hill. Two more drinks and we are pounding the pavements again. We lose Ken. He gives us all a big hug, tells us that his missus is at home waiting for him, that she gets moody when she doesn't get her fill of six inches, the randy woman. I'm thinking that six inches might be pushing it a bit. His eyes are bloodshot and his thinning hair is sticking up at one side. I suspect that his missus will have a headache tonight.

The light is fading. The offices are closing.

I sit upright in the corner of the bar, lips painted into a permanent smile. I'm floating on a cloud. The world is moving around me, but I stay still, watching from above. The rest of the group are talking – no – shouting, getting louder and louder with every syllable that they utter - but I'm not listening. Only certain words register. Words and phrases I hear and use every day of the week. *Touching base. Thinking outside the box.* You know the ones. I long to stand up and shout to the whole bar that the world is a wonderful, wonderful place! But my legs feel heavy, they feel lazy. They feel so, so different from the rest of me, which is peacefully drifting, floating…

The drinks keep coming, out of my control, against my will. I barely finish the one that I'm on when another is delivered, just like that. I press my hands down against the table, pull myself to my feet. I stumble into one suit, then another. They seem to be everywhere, getting in my way, blocking my path, all looking exactly the same. I reach my destination. I press my head against the cold, tiled wall. This is the life, I think.

I sit back down next to Paul, but I'm thinking of Katie. She looked beautiful this morning in her pinstriped black suit, long blonde hair tied back behind her neck. Smiled at me and planted a warm, wet kiss on my lips. Wished me all the best for the meeting. The image is just a hazy blur, but I can still feel that kiss on my lips, that wonderful taste. I turn to Paul, with his swanky suit and trendy haircut. The lad took me under his wing when I joined *360 Ltd.* He only started about six months before me but already he seemed so advanced, so senior. He has always looked after me, Paul. I decide here and now that I love the guy. He is the brother that I never had. I reach out and give him a kiss on the cheek. He raises his eyebrows, Roger Moore style, which is one of his traits, and somewhere in the background I hear Lawrence and Bruce laughing.

At some point Lawrence leaves, goes somewhere other than here. We are down to the three musketeers. I get to my feet (holding onto the table) and announce that I'm getting a round of shots in. I wish that I had a trumpet in my hand that I could blow into. It all deflates instantly, though. Paul gives me a hug and says count him out, sorry feller; that he needs to go too. Says he has a hot date. I bet he does. That smooth bastard gets all the chicks. I tell him to give her one for me. He tells me not to worry, he will give her two. There is no ongoing joke with Paul, I realise. He is too cool for any of that. He swaggers towards the door and, as if for good measure, catches the eye of a few hard bodies on his way out.

Now it is just two of us. Batman and Robin, Cagney and Lacey, Laurel and Hardy, the Chuckle brothers; whatever you want to call us, we are the last ones standing. Just me and my new best mate, Bruce. That is his name, isn't it? Bruce is talking, but God knows what about. His lips are moving. There is sound. I nod my head, up and down. *Yes sir, no sir, three bags full sir.* I start to say something but realise that the words make no sense, that I'm not even sure what I'm trying to say, and I'm not even sure why I'm bothering saying it. I know what I am thinking but the same words won't translate from my mind into my mouth. I shrug my shoulders and think, fuck it.

Bruce says that he is going to the bar. I understand. That is a language that I know all to well. He gets up, bumps into a suit. He stumbles into a table, almost falls into a group of girls. They look up, put their hands to their mouths; stifle their giggles. Bruce walks past the bar. He pushes the door open and walks out of that, too. I look out of the window and he is still walking. I bang on the glass with my knuckle, but he just keeps on walking.

Now it is just one. *The Lone Ranger*, whatever you want to call me, now it is just me standing.

I down the remains of my drink and leave. Check my watch. Nine thirty. I know exactly where I'm going. It's a mild night. There's an unmistakable aroma of pot in the air. Head towards Monument Station. The barriers aggressively flick open, looking for a fight. Almost get trapped. Bump into another suit. Catch the Circle Line. Fall into a seat. Smell the vomit. The floor has only just been cleaned. Look around. Suits stare intently at the floor, stare intently at the advertisements (for thrush and stool softeners); stare intently at *anything* but another suit. There is a big smile on my face. The motion of the train is making my head spin. I feel bile rising in my throat. I suspect that I am dribbling from the side of my mouth. I know that my forehead is sweating. Feels like two hundred and twenty stops. The recorded message finally announces South Kensington.

It takes me a while to find the right key, to put the key in the right way. The flat smells of freshly vacuumed carpets, of scented candles. It smells like home. Even though, it isn't. Not yet. We have talked about moving in together. It will happen soon. Now, though, I am a surprise. We are not supposed to meet until tomorrow night.

I push the bedroom door open. Katie is in the middle of the bed. Her long blonde hair is still tied primly behind her neck. She is still smiling. Her lips are pouted, ready for another warm, wet kiss. The kiss I can still taste from this morning. Only, now, sweat covers her brow. Her eyes are bloodshot. More significantly, she is on all fours, pert, gym-toned ass in the air. She stops what she is doing. We stare at each other. Time freezes. She does nothing. I do nothing. Look up. The hair is still slicked back. The smooth bastard gets all of the chicks. He is not talking his way out of this one. His mouth is open but no words are coming out. I wait. Paul shrugs his shoulders, as if to say, *no excuses mate, I've been caught.* I feel like an intruder. It is my cue to leave.

I am back outside. The night feels cold. I walk, but in no direction. I reach a bus stop; press my hand against the plastic glass, leaning at an angle. The bile returns. Flows through my throat. There is no stopping it. I am sick, again and again and again. I stare at the cracked pavement. It is covered with puke, shit and soggy chewing gum.

Suddenly the world does not seem like such a wonderful, wonderful place.

Chapter Two

I rather like my reputation, actually, that of a spoiled genius from the Welsh gutter, a drunk, a womanizer; it`s rather an attractive image – Richard Burton

There's a constant, uninvited noise somewhere in my bedroom, hiding somewhere in my bed. I know what it is; of course I do. Only I pretend I don't.

It's my alarm. Of course it is.

I'm afraid – no, I'm terrified - to open my eyes. The throbbing pain in that tiny gap just above the bridge of my nose is just like *way* too much. My eyelids are stuck together like glue. My mouth feels like sandpaper and my whole body is drenched in a salty, stale sweat. I force my eyes open. It feels like everything I see is magnified and out of focus. My wardrobe is just standing there, I know that, but to me it seems to be doing some sort of funky dance. I fumble for the phone. Turn off the noise. The noise in my head is still there, though, louder than ever now that it is no longer drowned out by the alarm. Positive thinking, I think. Tell myself that I'm a soldier, again and again, until I start to believe it. But no; I can hardly think at all, let alone think positively, or whatever it is. The TV is on. A breakfast show demonstrates how to cook the perfect Sunday roast, with thick gravy and crispy potatoes. Sick fills my throat.

I'm just overflowing with negativity.

I'm in morning hangover mode, which in itself is not unusual. It's become part of my normal routine. Wake up. Feel like shit. Only, somehow, today feels so much worse. There is something else, something that is *not* usual. There is something awful about today, I know, but I just can't remember what it is. So, instead, I go into automatic pilot mode.

Take my usual seat on the Streatham Common to London Bridge train. Smile at the lady who absolutely *always* sits opposite me. I'm certain that this woman has never even heard of annual leave. Flexi-time is a concept that belongs in a parallel universe. She gives a kind, knowing look, a look which says 'you look like hell, young man.' Maybe it's the layer of sweat on my forehead, maybe it is my flushed (still unblemished? – are you kidding me?) cheeks, maybe it's the bloodshot eyes. Hell, there are endless reasons why a stranger on a train would conclude that I look like shit. I glance at her. There are a few light lines around her eyes, what do they call it – crow's feet? Her skin looks slightly stretched, but she is undoubtedly still an attractive lady. The sort I would probably have a crack at if my mates weren't around. She is not a trophy wife, not like…like…anyway, I guess this lady is somewhere in her forties. She probably looks at me - all twenty-five years of me - and sees a young guy living the high life. If only she knew, I think, as the train shudders and my head pulsates.

I close my eyes. Think about yesterday. The meeting went well. Started at a steady pace and sped up like a train leaving the station, which is quite topical, really. The pace continued until the train almost derailed. I was the last man standing, too. It all sounded good to me.

I know what's wrong, though, of course I do. If I don't think about it, I reason, then, just maybe, it didn't happen. However, it's no good. The image of Katie on the bed, on all fours, keeps entering my mind, completely uninvited, totally unwanted. I try to push the image out, only it digs its heels into the floor and pushes back, even stronger.

I'm hyperventilating. The sweat seeps out of my alcohol-filled pores, leaving wet patches on my freshly laundered white shirt. I'm shaking. My shoes tap nervously on the floor. Everything feels unreal, like I'm trapped in a dream, or more accurately, a nightmare. My eyes are pressed tightly together, but I just know people are looking at me. I can't cope with them, not now, not ever. My panic hits a peak. And then, slowly but definitely, it begins to subside.

"Are you okay, dear?" the woman opposite asks. I've never heard her speak, not once in over two years. The train is coming into London Bridge. I cannot wait for it to stop so that I can get off; so that I can escape. This woman knows something is wrong. It's clear to see. For all the swagger and flash suit, she knows underneath I'm a mess.

I sniff. I smile. "I'm fine, thank you. Just a heavy night," I say, offering my best you-know-how-it-is look. I'm a party animal. I've been burning the candle at both ends. Good to let loose once on a while, etc, etc, whatever. She isn't convinced. She doesn't believe me for a second and, come to think of it, neither do I. But, thankfully, it doesn't really matter anymore. People are on their feet, and I can escape.

"I hope so, sweetheart. I will check again, though, just in case. Same place, same time, tomorrow," she smiles, sweetly.

"It's a date," I say, looking cool and collected, my hands shaking, my feet numb.

The *360 Ltd* office is on Monument Street, the other side of London Bridge. The building has twenty-three storeys, and we occupy floors sixteen and seventeen. Not much in the big scheme of things, really. I've never more than a moment's thought for what happens between floors one to fifteen and floors eighteen to twenty-three, and I'm pretty sure they don't care what goes on between floors sixteen and seventeen, either. I've been here three years now, and to me I feel like big news. Most of my mates are still back in Bridgend, working in shops or factories or living off their parents. I couldn't wait to get out, to be honest; to be someone, somewhere, so long as it wasn't back there. All the people back home need to know is that I work in the city, and that sounds pretty impressive, don't you think?

I say morning to the security guards. They say morning back. Take the lift to the seventeenth floor. Most of the desks are already occupied. Phones are ringing. Keyboards are tapping. Photocopiers are doing whatever photocopiers do; photocopy, I guess. Take a deep breath. Paul will already be here, acting the big man, already organising the next big meeting.

"Morning, Nick. How was the meeting yesterday?"

It's Steph, PA to the real boss man, Max Vaughan. Twenty-three, straight out of University (Masters, naturally), slim body, curves where curves should be (traditionally, because we are all different, I can accept that), bubbly and flirtatious. Of course, all the guys in the office want to bend her over the photocopier, and not to do whatever photocopiers do. Of course, she has a boyfriend. Of course, he is older, and richer. A Director at *Credit Suisse*, or somewhere like that, apparently. Little bastard.

I decide to put on a performance, which I've actually become good at doing, when I choose to. I've been doing it for long enough; copying Paul. The difference is, though, as I've found out, with Paul it isn't a performance.

"It was the crème de le crème of meetings, Steph," I say, elaborately removing my Versace jacket and just about managing to flash my best, minty-fresh smile, hoping that I managed to brush out all the sick from last night. "Relevant information was delivered concisely and with an appropriate level of enthusiasm. Questions were asked and answers were provided. *Lasocte* were left in no doubt that *360 Ltd* are the company to drive them forward in the current climate."

Steph leans across my desk. She has painted nails. "My hero," she coos.

I'm turning on my PC, adjusting my seat level, when she delivers the deadly line. "Oh, Nick, when you get the chance, Max wants to see you in his office, please."

She is being casual. Playing it down. The big boss man wants to see me. Now, this could be good new or bad news, but either way, it's definitely scary-as-fuck news.

I know that the 'when you get the chance' line is just that - a line. When Max Vaughan wants to see you in his office, you drop everything else you are doing and go and see him, even if you happen to be delivering your wife's baby at the time.

I knock on the door. He bellows for me to enter.

"Ah, Nick, come in, come in," he says, standing up. "Take a seat, dear boy. Thank you for coming to see me so quickly. It's just a chat, nothing serious."

Good timing, you silly old bastard, I think. Calling me in for 'just a chat' when my head is about to explode, when my stomach is like a tumble dryer, whizzing around and around. "My pleasure, Mr Vaughan," I say.

"Please, I've told you before Nick that I prefer to be called Max," he laughs, even though it's obvious he much prefers to be called Mr Vaughan.

The office smells of vapour rub, which isn't a surprise, really, as Max always smells of vapour rub. I wonder where he rubs it and why. Then, immediately, I try *not* to wonder where he rubs it and why, not with my stomach feeling like it does today.

"Paul is not in the office today. I don't think that he will be in for the next couple of weeks, Nick. I spoke to him personally." He adjusts his square glasses. "Have you noticed anything up with Paul recently, Nick?"

Apart from his dick inside my missus? I think.

"No," I say, trying to sound concerned. "I hope everything is okay?"

Max removes the lid off his fountain pen and then puts it back on again, and I wonder why he took it off in the first place.

"Unfortunately, Nick, it appears that Paul is feeling the pressure of driving *360 Limited* through the current climate. It happens to quite a few of the main players in this industry, determined to take on all of the responsibility. Paul is going to be a massive loss for the time that he is away, Nick."

I try my best to keep a neutral face. I clench my teeth together and then bite into my upper lip. Regardless, I may as well have 'bullshit' pencilled in big capital letters on my shiny, perspiring forehead. Paul is the one who has called in sick, and Paul is the one being portrayed as the injured war hero. It's my Goddamn girlfriend who has been feeling all the pressure that Paul has to offer.

"I'm sorry to hear that, Max," I say, with all the sincerity I can muster. "Really, I am."

Max looks serious, like he has reverted into fighting mode. "You know what this means, Nick?" he asks.

I think for a moment. No, I have no idea what the fuck this means, none whatsoever. "I think so," I offer, hopefully.

"It means, Nick," he continues, almost spitting out the words, "that as Paul's partner in crime, I want you to shoulder some more of the responsibilities. Don't let Paul carry too much." He looks at me closely now, really examines me. I can't believe for a second that he can be impressed with what he sees. "This is a real opportunity for you to show your value, Nick."

I inhale the vapour rub. So what it means, Max, is that Paul has gone off sick for working too hard and you want *me* to work harder so that *I* can go off sick instead? I press my fingers against the underside of his desk, and they stick against some chewing gum (surprising, as the room is only used for 'important' meetings).

"I understand, Max," I say. "And I am grateful for the opportunity. I can assure you of one thing. You can count on me."

Max becomes strangely energetic (especially for such an old bastard). He shuffles papers over his big wooden desk and offers his big, hairy hand, which I duly shake. It feels hot and sticky, as if he has just applied vapour rub. "Good man, good man," he says. "I knew that I could rely on you!"

Back at my desk, I look for an easy ride. No distractions. No phone calls. No paperwork thrown in my direction. I know that I have to write up the minutes from yesterday's meeting, but it's easy work.

I bang forcefully on the keyboard, making sure everyone within the vicinity knows that I'm at least doing *something*. I delete what I've written. Start again, and then delete that too. Steph comes over. Now, she *is* a welcome distraction. I could do with a break.

"Everything okay, Nick?" she asks, leaning slightly forward over my desk. She is wearing a lacy black bra, and she subtly pushes her breasts together with her arms. I notice how green her eyes are. I'm trying hard not to look anywhere else.

"Absolutely perfect," I say, clasping my hands behind my neck. "Between you and me, Max has just given me some extra responsibility. Quite an opportunity, even if I do say so myself." I give her a knowing wink.

"Ooh, watch you!" she says, smiling. There is a tiny blot of lipstick on the side of her mouth. "You're a proper boy racer, aren't you?"

I'm mesmerised by the movements of her lips, by the way she twists her mouth in all different shapes and directions. I think of Katie, with her big undeniable blow job lips, and wonder whether they were wrapped around Paul's dick last night. Of course they were, I think, who am I trying to kid? The bile returns to my throat. I'm so absorbed that I've no idea when it is that Steph moves away from my desk.

I manage to survive till lunchtime, and I'm straight down the pub, in like Flynn, straight to *The Venturer,* a little bar on Gracechurch Street where I've never seen anyone from work. I order a gin and take a seat. I know all too well that gin is a depressive, people are always very keen to tell you things that you don't need to know, aren't they? I want to be depressed right now, though.

There are groups of rowdy suits in each corner. I am the singleton reading the *Financial Times*. Only, I don't have a *Financial Times* and I'm not reading. I order another drink. They are going down well. Numbs the mind. Eases the nausea. If I can only drink enough, I reason, I might start feeling normal again. If only I didn't have to go back to work.

I check my phone. Seven missed calls from Katie. No text messages. No voicemail. I go to call her. I go to text her. Realise I've no idea what I want to say. *Sorry that I caught you in an uncompromising position with Action Man last night, can we please resume our Ken and Barbie relationship?* I think about phoning somebody else, anybody else. I cannot think of anyone, apart from my mum, and how can a grown man like me phone his mum when he's feeling upset? I know hundreds of people in London, I have never been so popular, and yet right now the only people I can think of are clients, people I wine and dine to secure my bonus. None of them are going to be interested in my personal problems.

I leave the bar and head to the department store. Buy a bottle of Jack Daniels. The idea of surviving the afternoon sober seems, right now, just a bit crazy.

I hardly do any work in the next few hours. I remember my assurances to Max that he can count on me. Like fuck he can, I think, the silly old bugger. I dawdle and scribble and take discreet sips of whisky from the glass I've hidden behind my PC. It soothes both my chest and my racing thoughts. I manage to complete the minutes from the meeting. I email them to the appropriate parties, and copy Paul in. I promptly receive calls from Lawrence, Ken and Bruce, thanking me for the minutes, thanking me for yesterday. They all tell me that Paul is one crazy son of a bitch. I consider telling them about my trauma, about my heartache and stress, but I don't want to burden them and, more importantly, I don't think they would want to know.

Steph pulls up a chair at my desk. Her face is flushed, pink in the cheeks and nose. Her mascara is blotched. She needs somebody to talk to, that bit is obvious, and she's chosen me.

The drink is starting to take effect. I'm sure I'm just topping up from yesterday and last night and maybe, if truth be told, from last week, too. Steph is talking to me, whatever, but I'm not really listening. I consider whether I would stand a chance with her, now that I'm back on the market. I'm a catch, I guess. I tick most of the important boxes that women look for, don't I? I have a good job in the city, I'm not totally ugly and I earn a decent package. But then I dismiss the thought. She wouldn't be interested in me, not when that smarmy bastard boyfriend of hers is way richer than I am.

I stare at her lips. Her mouth is quite small really, a perfect circle, but her lips are plump and full. There's a cute little freckle on her cheek (if you were polite you'd probably call it a beauty spot, and if you were not polite you'd call it a mole) that I've not noticed before. No doubt I've probably been too busy staring at her tits, which just always seem to be looking straight back at me. I've a mad compulsion to lick the freckle, to see whether it comes off on my tongue. I worry that I might be dribbling from the side of my mouth, just like I did on the pillow last night. I consciously order myself to at least *try* and listen to whatever it is she is saying.

"Max gives me all this work and sets all of these unrealistic deadlines, I tell you, Nick, and do I ever get a real thank you, I ask you? I think not," she says. Her bloodshot eyes have morphed into full, plopping tears now. I'm starting to get a bit self-conscious. There are a few dolly birds peering over their monitors, soaking up the possible gossip. They'll be in the break area after, no doubt, bitching. I know they'll be expecting me to do something, to put an arm around Steph, or to provide some supportive, consoling words. Do *something*, at least. All I can think, though, is that I need some more drink. There is sweat on my forehead and it's hot and sticky and uncomfortable and my hair is starting to feel itchy, too.

I go to put my hand on her shoulder, but then decide against it. It doesn't feel quite right. Instead I tap her on the arm. It is more of a prod, really, with my middle finger.

Steph gets a tissue from her handbag and blows her nose, then wipes the tears from her eyes with the same tissue. I can't help thinking that she is rubbing snot over her face. The thought is a distraction. Steph sits upright, removing her elbows from the desk. She is pulling herself together. I can almost sense her counting to ten, taking deep, steady breathes. I wonder whether she does yoga.

"Thank you for listening, Nick," she says. "I knew I could rely on you. I feel much, much better now." Steph squeezes my hand.

"No problem," I mutter. "It's really no problem at all. I don't think I did much at all," I continue, coyly.

Soon as she is gone, I flee from my desk and head straight for the toilets, the miniature bottle of Jack Daniels hidden in my pocket. I lock the door to the cubicle and park my backside down on the toilet seat. Open the bottle. Pull my head back and take a big swig. There is only about a third of the bottle left, I notice. May as well finish it, I reason. My cheeks are hot. My fingers tingle. I walk out of the cubicle with a new, confident swagger, just like that bastard Paul does, and throw the empty bottle into the trash can on the way out.

Back at my desk, I'm a livelier, more positive version of my former self. I can be supportive. I can be funny. I can bring a smile to a girl's face. I urgently bang away at the keyboard.

We all appreciate the hard work you put in Steph. You should tell Mr Big Boss Man to stick his vapour rub where the sun doesn't shine!

I look at Steph, wait for her to open her email. It flashes on her screen when she receives a message, a red devil with a twisting tail, or something. I know, I've seen it often enough. Nothing happens. No message. Max comes out of his office. He is walking towards me. No, he is *pacing* towards me. No, on thirds thoughts, he is *charging* towards me, and I know what he wants, before he even opens his mouth, before he even utters a fucking word. I'm sure that the Big Boss Man, Max Vaughan, did not find the email that was intended for Steph very supportive or funny. Right now, the Big Boss Man definitely does not have a smile on his face.

"Go fuck yourself, Max!" I shout, like a little terrier dog getting in the first bark before the big Alsatian dog bites him. I stand up and walk out of *360 Ltd* for the last time.

At least, I think, as I catch the lift from the seventeenth floor and say goodnight to the security guards, who say goodnight back, I can tell everyone back home that I wasn't sacked.

***

I'm with Den and we are crossing the bridge over the river, moving away from the town centre. I'm carrying a bag of chips and I'm eating them with a blue plastic fork, and the flimsy white paper, stained with vinegar, blows madly in the wind.

Somebody is waking towards us from the opposite direction, on the pavement by the river. The tall, wiry figure seems familiar, but I'm not sure why and I can't make him out. As the person comes closer, the figure becomes more and more familiar.

It is Sam.

I haven't seen him for ages and I feel real exhilaration. The face is angular and the cheekbones are moulded. He looks just like he always did. Sam holds out his hand and I hug him. I ask him where he has been and he says you know how it is, this and that, just needed to sort out a few things. It all feels strange, like it can't be so, and yet I think why it is so strange, and so I shrug my shoulders, and the three of us are the best of friends again, just like we were just before that final year in school, down on the beach. We cross another bridge and continue walking past the sloping roof of the leisure centre and on towards Newbridge Fields.

There is a game of rugby on the first pitch, and it is a big game too, with groups of supporters shouting and cheering loudly on both touchlines. We reach the stones which stand upright in a circle - they must be at least five feet high - and I count fourteen of them, as I always do, with an extra one in the middle. My black leather shoes sink into the soggy grass.

Sam runs up ahead. He looks dainty and nimble, just like a dancer on ice. I notice for the first time that he is wearing grey flannel trousers just a little too short and a white shirt which hangs loose over his belt, and a lopsided tie. He is wearing his uniform, the one from school. It seems bizarre but everything about today is bizarre and so maybe he is just going to one of those parties you hear about, or something. And he is skipping along now, literally bouncing on his feet. All these years of worrying about my friend, and here he is, looking like the happiest guy in the world.

Den is chasing after him now, with big cumbersome strides. I'm intrigued and mystified by all the activity at the park today. All of the pitches are being used; there are two football matches and another rugby match. The little remaining vacant space, by the steeply sloping concrete steps and alongside the old wooden cricket pavilion, is taken up by dogs running freely round in circles, chasing after each other. It is a perfect day.

I know exactly where Sam is heading. He is running towards the rope swing. He increases his pace and, without a moment's hesitation, he jumps out into the middle of the river and takes hold of the rope, which hangs from a thick sturdy tree branch. He swings back and forth with just one hand on the rope. With the other hand he waves to me and Den. Sam jumps from the rope and lands perfectly on the muddy river bank. Den jumps out into the river and his grip is firmer and he is less fluid.

I want a go and surely it is my turn next, but as I take backward steps to prepare for my launch, Sam gets in there quick and he jumps out into the middle of the river. Only this time he does not swing effortlessly back and forth. He sinks down, and he screams like a girl as he crashes against the side of the bank.

Den and I are laughing so much so that Den lies down on the grass, in a fit of hysterics, his legs kicking and flailing wildly. I climb down the sloping river edge, but there is no grip on my black shoes and I slip and slide until I reach the bottom. I locate the rope but Sam is not attached to it. It suddenly feels so dark and cold down here. I shout out for Sam but my voice seems drowned out and I can hardly hear myself.

I climb up the rope but my arms feel skinnier and my body heavier than I ever remember it. I reach the top and it is raining now and the sky is black and bleak. I look for Den but he is no longer lying on the floor. The games of football have finished and the dogs have gone home and now it is just me in a dark endless playing field.

I scream at the top of my voice and it is then, when I wake up covered in a cold sweat, I realise that I have been dreaming.

I know that it is a dream because Sam has been missing for the last seven years, and in real life, he never comes back.

Chapter Three

My act is very educational. I heard a man leaving the other night saying 'well, that taught me a lesson' – Ken Dodd

It is no good. I just can't stand it any more! I need to get out of the house.

It's no good. I just can't stand it anymore! I just have to get out of the house before I go stark raving mad.

Eleven in the morning is usually when I take my first break – white coffee with two digestive biscuits, thank you. At eleven today, though, I am still in bed. I stare, zombie-like, at the TV screen, which has been left on mute, again. I just can't think of anything that is worthwhile getting up for. In the end, I pull myself out of bed because I just can't face lying there anymore.

But after sitting on the sofa with my balls hanging out of my boxers for about thirty minutes, casually flicking the channels of the TV, channels dominated by cooking programmes, personal injury adverts and antiques shows, I decide that either I go back to bed or I go out.

And it's not a bad day, I guess, for this country. The pavements are dry, and there is only the odd cloud in the sky. I walk past the common. There are a few mothers pushing baby buggies and a couple of old men on benches drinking cans of lager. I imagine this is what it is like every day, another world that exists while I'm usually in work. It is not really a world that I want to become part of. I pass the Crown pub, which I guess is officially my local, although I pretend it isn't. I pass it in the morning and in the evening on the way to and from the train station. There's usually a sign outside advertising such excitements as Saturday night karaoke and Tuesday afternoon bingo. I always pass it. I have never, ever been inside.

And so, as this does not feel like a normal day, I go inside.

It is busier than I expected. There are the usual

singletons, loser old men drinking warm, stale bitter, reading the Sun paper, but three or four tables are occupied by groups of five and more. Even older men, with skin like old newspaper, bald heads and glazed faded expressions. The only light comes from the spring sun which seeps weakly through the stained window. This place is way below my normal level; it's the sort of place where you wipe your feet on the way out, but today that sort of works in my favour. I feel confident that, however sad and helpless and depressed I am today, I am not going to feel out of place here. So, I stay for a drink.

For the second time in two days, I am the single guy in a pub. I'm going to get myself a reputation. I take a seat in the corner on a battered, wobbly wooden chair. The corners of the pub are vacant. It is only £2.70 for a pint of bitter, which is just unknown in the city. It tastes cold and fresh. I am sure that I can smell cabbage from the kitchen, but it seems to fit in with the rest of the place quite well. I go to check that my tie is straight, that I am not letting the side down, but realise I am only wearing a tee shirt and that, maybe more importantly, nobody cares.

There is a man two tables down sat on his own, just like me. I recognise him, and wonder why. It feels I know him, like the lady on the train. I know where. It is from the same pub, the same seat. I see him through the window every night on the way home from work. He is sometimes alone, sometimes with others, but he is always there, always drinking a pint of Guinness. The guy has uneven, pockmarked skin and a full mop of grey, curly hair. He is probably about sixty-five, maybe older, who knows. I wonder whether they keep a glass behind the bar for him.

He looks up from his drink and catches me looking. I glance away. He probably thinks I'm looking at him and thinking *what a loser*. Which, of course, I am.

I hear him speaking. To me.

"I recognise you, laddie," he says, almost accusingly. "You usually walk past every night looking like Charlie Sheen straight from Wall Street! Not in work today?"

He does not sound like I expected. I am not sure what I

expected him to sound like, but not this. He has a high-pitched Scouse accent, but then I guess all Scousers are high pitched. *Calm down, calm down, I only stole your car*, I jest to myself.

I find myself at the bar buying a lager for me and a pint of Guinness for him, which kind of surprises me. I sit down on the chair opposite, not that I've been invited. He doesn't seem put out, and he thanks me for the drink.

"Don't work anymore," I say, taking a casual sip from my lager and giving an even more casual shrug of my shoulders. He looks at me, absorbing the information. His eyes are blue and watery. He breaks into a smile. Then he starts laughing. The guy finds the information hilarious. For no reason, I laugh too.

"So what's your name, then? I keep going to call you Charlie."

For some reason, I always ponder whether to give my full name in these circumstances. I remember this time Den and I got stopped by a policeman, in the early hours of the morning after a night out in Cardiff. We both had traffic cones in our hands and were carrying them across the River Taff, down by the Millennium Stadium. We were going to take them home with us as a souvenir for the night out, as you do. This copper really took exception, though, and started shouting at us, making a scene. The guy was probably getting a power kick out of it, I thought. He shouted at me, told me that he wanted my name, and my full name at that. I told him I was Nick Evans.

"Do you have a middle name, son?" he bellowed.

"Yes," I replied.

"I said I want your *full* name!" he screeched.

So I told him that I was Nicholas Harold Evans, and now I consider giving the same response to this stranger in this pub.

"Nick," I eventually offer.

"How did that happen, Nick?" he asks. The nosy git really wants to know, too.

I try to tell him as little as possible, to leave the main nitty-gritty details out, but I end up telling him everything. How I found my girlfriend shagging my best mate, how I told my boss to go fuck himself. Everything. His face turns beetroot red. Tears run down his rough, stubbly cheeks. He cannot stop laughing. Eventually he gets up out of his chair and says that he will get us both a drink. "You need it, lad. In a bit," he says.

I find myself checking my phone, which I have been trying to avoid. Four missed calls and five messages. Never been so popular. There is a message from Katie saying that we need to talk, and another from Paul saying exactly the same thing. I wonder whether they drafted the message together, the dumb idiots. I switch off the phone off and put it in my pocket.

"Right pair we are, eh Taffy," the guy says, returning from the bar. I guess we are. Only, he looks happier than me. There is a red stain on his blue woolly jumper (probably ketchup, I think, or maybe baked beans), and he looks like he has not had a wash all week, but definitely, he looks happier than me.

My new friend asks me whether I speak Welsh, and I give the same answer that I always give, word for word. He asks me to say something to him in Welsh.

"Rwy'n chwarae pel-droed," I say.

"What does that mean?"

"I play football."

"And do you?" he asks.

"No," I say.

His face suggests he isn't quite sure what to make of me. He asks which part of Wales I'm from.

"Bridgend," I reply.

He pauses for a moment, wondering where he knows the name from. It suddenly dawns on him after a moment, as it usually does.

"Isn't that where all those…."

"Yes," I interrupt. "But it's not actually such a bad place," I continue, and I mean it, I think, though I'm not sure whether I'm trying to convince myself that I do. "The people are as friendly as they come, and it's really gorgeous down the coast."

He takes in the information, and I'm guessing by the

perplexed look on his face that he's probably wondering why I bothered moving away if it was all that wonderful.

"So how did you end up like this then?" I ask.

His watery eyes narrow. There is an extra crease on his forehead (and there's hardly room for another). "How do you mean?" he asks.

"You know," I say, looking around the pub, feeling a bit awkward. "Like *this?"*

"Like *this*?" he asks again, looking confused. Oh God, I think. I wish I had a shovel.

Fortunately the guy breaks into a smile. "I'm only kidding, kiddo," he says. His laugh is surprisingly deep. "You mean, how did my life get this fucked up?"

"No, no," I protest, putting my hands by my chest, but he laughs some more.

"I'm on a wind up, kid," he says. "I had it all, you know. Good job, sexy girlfriend. Came home one day, like, and found her cheating on me, didn't I? Gobbling on six inches of prime meat. Was one of my mates, for fuck's sake! It got me drinking. I told my boss to fuck his job, like, didn't I? Well, that was thirty years ago. I've been sat here ever since."

He looks proper miserable now. He takes another sip of Guinness, probably to weaken the awful memories. I absorb the information. Makes me depressed. Something hits home. "You mean," I say, "it's just like what's happened to me?"

It is his turn to think now. I can almost see a light bulb flashing above his hunched right shoulder "Yeah, I guess it is, lad. Fucks sake, like!"

We both stare absently at our half-empty glasses. My life is fucked, I think. I'm going to end up like this sad old loser. I glance at the man again, this stranger. His weathered old face breaks into another smile. "I'm only kidding, lad," he says, slamming his hand down on the table, laughing again. "You've been shagging too many sheep. Your brain's gone to mush."

I know that relief is etched all over my face. "Okay then, Ken Dodd," I say, trying to control my nerves. "What *did* happen?"

The guy takes a long gulp of his drink. His blue eyes flicker nervously. "Well, the first bit is true enough. No bullshitting there. I did have it all, and more. Worked as an analyst in the city, didn't I? I took home six figures, and that's when six figures actually meant something. This was back in the eighties, when yuppies were all the rage."

It's hard to take in that this guy could have been a player in the city, but I know that he is not bullshitting me. I've never earned three figures, although I like to give the impression I do. His head is bowed. There is a perfect pink circle at the back, with big tufts of hair either side. He does not want to look me in the eye. I say nothing; just wait for him to continue.

"I guess I just got burnt out, lad. Too much drink. Just too much everything! Got to the point where I needed a drink, just so that I could face going to work. Dabbled in the white stuff for breakfast. Fuck shredded wheat, this was the eighties. The thought of the office brought me out in a hot sweat. I started losing my nerves, going real crazy."

This part is not so hard to take in. I've seen it before. You keep blowing until the balloon bursts. And it's a long way to fall when you are at the top. Blah de blah. "So they axed you?" I ask, possibly a little inconsiderately.

He looks up. There are red blotches underneath his eyes. His bottom lip is quivering. "No, I didn't give them the chance. I got out, like. Told my boss to fuck his job, didn't I? That bit is right. I guess the only part that of the first story that wasn't true, lad, is I didn't come home and find my girlfriend chomping on some cock, thank fuck for that."

Yeah, I think, what sort of a loser would walk in on his girlfriend like that? I almost envy the guy. His story is sad, but it isn't as sad as mine.

"So you still need the drink then?" I ask. "Couldn't face ever going back to work?"

We are interrupted by the barmaid coming around with a plate full of sandwiches. He takes two, then three, then four. I think, you greedy old bastard, then I take just as many. There are ham and cheese and chicken, all in white bread and smothered in butter.

"Cheers, Denise, pet, you're an angel," the guy says, his mouth full of sandwich.

Denise looks happy as Larry. Her cheeks are flushed red and I am sure there is an even extra bounce in her full, plump bosom. "My pleasure, Harry," she says, displaying a row of crooked front teeth. Now Harry looks happy as Larry. I realise I have only just learnt his name. It feels like a long time I have known him before knowing his name.

"So, Harry," I say, "why you always here?"

Harry is not going to be rushed. He finishes his third and then his fourth sandwich, before even attempting to speak. He holds up his yellow finger as if to say, *hold on a second*, and then he puts down his finger and sticks another sandwich in his mouth and then holds up his finger again. No wonder the guy is usually sitting on his own, I think, but I don't really mind.

"August 28th 1989 was my last day in work, kiddo. I remember it well. It was a Thursday and the sun was shining. Fanny everywhere, I tell you. I told my boss to go fuck himself at just gone three in the afternoon, and on the way home, I stopped here. It was the first time, like. I was usually in the yuppie bars in the city. And you know, for the first time in who knows how long, I felt myself. Nobody judging me. It wasn't the same high as the coke, but it felt more natural."

I know *exactly* what he means, course I do. It frightens me, though. I don't want to turn into this guy, telling my story to some young pretender thirty years down the line.

"And I guess you never could face going back to work?" I ask, finishing off my drink. Harry still has some dregs left. I wish he would hurry up so that I can go to the bar and get another. Again, the guy is in no hurry.

"That's the funny thing," he says, wiping his mouth with his dirty sleeve. "I was thirty-nine when I quit my job, and I worked in the city straight from school. You needed big balls in those days, not big qualifications, to get on. And my balls," he said, taking a handful of them underneath the table, "were big! I earned more than I could ever spend, like, so I had a small fortune in the bank. For a good few years in work

I always felt that I needed the drink, the coke, just to keep going. But that kind of went when I left my job. I'll be honest with you, I could have been back in a top job within a couple of weeks of quitting, I felt better than I had in years, know what I mean?"

I wait for him to continue, but he just stops and drains his glass. He is waiting for me to ask him the obvious question. "So why didn't you go back to work, Harry?" I ask.

He looks me in the eye. I notice a slight twitch in his ruddy cheek. He takes a deep breath. "I guess you could analyse it all day and do a big Freudian thing, like. But the bottom line is, I've never wanted to go back. I've never been happier than I am here."

I go to the bar and get another round in. We are joined by a few of his mates. They all have grey hair and yellow fingers and brown teeth but each of them has a story to tell. They are the type I usually take a sideways step to avoid walking down the street. I just keep on laughing, though. One round turns to another and the light is starting to dim outside and now people are coming in from work. I am feeling lightheaded and decide to make a move.

Harry shakes my hand. His grip is firm and he holds my eye contact. "You aren't so bad, you know. At first I weren't so sure, but when you are yourself, you aren't so bad, you know? Good luck, anyway, Taffy," he growls.

Outside, there are no longer any single mothers pushing prams, but the old guys are still there drinking cans of Tennent's. Only they look even older, even sadder. I put the key in the door upside down, fumbling with the lock. There is still nobody in. My housemates are probably enjoying Friday night drinks, like the rest of the working population.

My mind is already made up. I have never been more certain about anything in my whole life. I leave a note for my housemates, explaining why I'm doing it. I pick up the phone. It rings the other end. I hear a familiar voice.

"Dad," I say. "I'm coming home."

Chapter Four

I love the opportunity to come back home and sing in Wales –
Katherine Jenkins

Southerndown, just outside Bridgend, South Wales

"Thank you, Charles," my mum says. My dad, Charles, has just delivered tea in her favourite china cup. "I don't know what I'd do without you, dear, really I don't," she continues, shaking her head from side to side. My mum says this every time my dad delivers tea in her favourite china cup, which, on average, is about three or four times a night.

It's Sunday night at seven o'clock. We have just finished dinner, or tea, as we call it back in Bridgend. Toasted scones, a cup of tea, pickled onions and salt and vinegar crisps. It's the same every Sunday at seven.

It has been less than twenty-four hours since my Dad picked me up from Bridgend Station in his trusty old blue Ford Fiesta. The Paddington to Swansea train ran like clockwork, as it tends to. He was already waiting for me when I arrived, as I thought he would be, in his usual grey slacks and smart shirt, initially just an outline in the car park. He looked shorter than I remembered him, but I think that every time I see him. The truth is he has never been very big. Maybe it was just that he seemed bigger because I was younger and smaller. I cannot imagine that he is shrinking – not yet – he is only early sixties. His hair was swept across his forehead and there were a couple of red indents where he had been wearing his glasses. He shook my hand and put my luggage in the boot, all three suitcases of it. We manoeuvred down Nolton Street, veering round some drunks, out of the town and towards the coast. The heating in the car was on high. The seats were comfortable. I felt relaxed.

"Your mum is worried about you, son," my dad said, and it was all he did say during the four or so mile journey.

I sit in the lounge with Mum. My dad has departed to the kitchen to do the dishes. He does not need to be asked. My Auntie Jean once asked why they didn't get a dishwasher. My mum laughed. "Why would I want to buy a dishwasher when I already have the best dishwasher in the whole world?" she asked, patting my dad on his knee. I remembered looking at my dad, who said nothing, and thinking that he really doesn't want a dishwasher either. We can hear the faint sound of my father methodically washing in the background, the clinking of plates as they are placed on the drainer.

"Your dad is ever so worried about you, Nicholas," my mum says, again shaking her head, which she has been doing a whole lot since I've been home. "He was pottering around in his shed all day yesterday. The poor man didn't know what to do with himself."

My dad is always pottering around in the shed. There is nothing new with this. The shed is only a little green wooden thing in the far corner of the garden, and it has been there for as long as I can remember. I haven't been in it since I was a kid. It would somehow feel like I was rummaging through his underwear drawer, not that I know what that would feel like. People link my dad to his shed. "And how is Charles?" they ask. "Is he still pottering around in his shed?" Nobody is really sure what he actually does in there, although the official stance is that he paints.

"You're twenty-five now, Nicholas," my mum states, as if this would be news to me. "I should know," she continues, emitting a laugh. "I was there when you were born!"

I know my mother is going to drift, and my own attention wanders. I glance around the room. Not much has changed over the years, I consider. The thick red and white carpet (vacuumed every day) is still the same. The walnut grandfather clock (dusted every day) stands tall and proud in the corner. The fireplace is filled with all sorts of ornaments, such as a mahogany elephant with a twisting trunk, and an ugly bust of Queen Victoria. It is a curious blend of old and new, however. The flat screen television must be at least fifty inches. The Samsung laptop on the mantelpiece has only just hit the shelves.

"Twenty-first of May, 1986 at six in the morning," my mum continues. "I was in the Heath for three whole days! The nurses were on my Christmas card list, I was there that long. And people ask me why I only had one child," she laughs. "I always say that after my Nicholas, never again." Her voice quivers just a little.

My father returns from the kitchen. "I was just looking out of the window, Deborah," he says, as he carefully places himself down in his chair by the television, "and thinking how nice the garden looks, love."

My mum looks ecstatic. She always does, every time my dad says this. Every time anyone says it, in fact. The house may only be a three bedroom semi-detached (with a garage and a long sloping drive, mind you) but it has an expansive garden both front and back, which always looks absolutely amazing, with an immaculate green lawn (mowed methodically by my father) and an elaborate array of flowers of all different colours (carefully nurtured by my mother). "Well, I've always been the one with the green fingers!" my mum laughs, and my dad happily nods his head like Churchill the dog.

Mum finishes her tea. A reminder flashes up on the TV, and my father turns over. *The Antiques Road Show* begins. There is a moment of silence. My mother's face turns sour. I wish that I had taken the opportunity to fill the silence.

"I can't believe Kate has left you, Nick," my mother says. Her face is a picture of concern. "You said that she ran off with your best friend, Paul? I hope that you treated her right, Nicholas? What would have made her do such a thing?"

This is no surprise at all. Of course, the fact that my girlfriend was caught in bed with my best friend would be my fault. My mother spoke to Katie as much as she spoke to me. I phoned my mum every Sunday evening, at six o'clock on the dot, making sure that she'd be finished before tea at seven. The phone would always ring for quite some time before my dad picked up the phone. My dad *always* picked up the phone. It was as if my mum didn't make a link between the phone ringing and someone being on the other end of the line.

"Hello, Dad," I'd say, "it's Nick."

My dad always seemed surprised that it was me, even though I called at the same time every week. He'd call out to my mum that I was on the phone, and I'd hear her saying oh what a nice surprise.

"Hello Nick, you are you?" he'd ask.

"Good thanks, Dad, how are you?"

"Can't complain, can't complain. Do you want to speak to your mum?"

"Yes please."

My mum would already be stood next to my dad, waiting for the receiver. She'd talk quickly and excitedly about my work, what I had been eating (are you looking after yourself, Nick?), my housemates, about my absolutely everything. She knew the names of the people I worked with, what shops were on my street. At some point, she would ask, "and so, Nick, how is Kate?" I'd explain in great detail exactly how Katie was. There would be a pause. I would let it drag, deliberately, just to see how long she would wait before asking. "And is she there, Nick?" I'd pass the phone and my mother would gossip with Katie for a good thirty minutes about the goings on in her Monday night village committee meetings, her Wednesday afternoon yoga classes, about her absolute everything.

"I'm going to miss our little chats," my mum says, and I'm almost certain she gives me an accusing look.

I go to change the subject, ask her about the neighbours (my parents used to be best friends with Ken and Deidre next door – yes, Ken and Deidre - until they built a conservatory which overlooked their garden two years ago, and they haven't spoken since), but my mother is on a roll now. "And you had such a good job at *360 Ltd,* Nick. You said Max Vaughan was very impressed with your work, that you secured new business with Legal and General and ABN Amro. And now how are you going to get a job in Bridgend? There are no jobs here, dear."

That's the thing with my mum. She gives the impression that she lives in a bubble, a secluded, sheltered village life, but in reality she is annoyingly clued up about most things.

She knew more about my job, for example, than I did. If ever I was to go sick, I honestly believe she could have stood in for me and probably done a better job, too.

When I was earning a decent wage in London, I'm sure my mum never said to anyone how good I was doing, but now I'm back and unemployed, she never fails to remind me.

"Nicholas has qualifications and experience, love," my father says. "He will find a job here soon enough."

I really must be in trouble, I consider, if Dad feels it necessary to back me up. He is a man of few words, anyway, but I've never ever seen him stand up to Mum. He may wear the trousers in the house, but she sure tells him which ones he can wear. I've always imagined that most kids look up to their dad as the biggest, strongest man in the world, that is until they grow up and realise that he is just like any other average Joe who works Monday to Friday and cleans his car on Sunday. But with my dad I've never even been afforded that delusion. I can't pretend that he has ever been a hero to me, to be honest.

My mother hasn't taken any notice of him. She is distracted by a nineteenth century pocket watch on the television. My eyes scan the room. On the bookcase next to the television stand, my eyes look over latest copies of *Heat* and *Hello* magazine and a hardback copy of Trinny and Susannah – *What you Wear Can Change Your Life*.

I go into the kitchen and run the tap. I haven't had a drink in a couple of days and though I can't really say I've needed one, I've sure been guzzling a fair few glasses of water. It is only eight-something and already I don't know what to do with myself. This place really doesn't seem big enough for me anymore. Already I'm missing London.

My dad comes into the kitchen. He is wearing his slippers, and is as quiet as a mouse. I hadn't even heard him come in. He is holding a piece of paper with a telephone number and a web site scrawled on it. It is my mum's writing.

"Your mum is worried about you bringing some money into the house, son," he says, quietly. "She has looked up how you can make a claim for Jobseekers. If you could look at it tomorrow for me please, otherwise she won't get a wink of sleep."

Wow, I think, I've only been home two minutes and already they are trying to get money out of me! I know that my dad doesn't feel comfortable asking me, though, and that my mum really won't sleep a wink until I've got something sorted. She once said that if she didn't have anything to worry about, she'd worry about that, and she was right, too.

"Okay, Dad," I say, taking the slip of paper from him.

The music for the *Antiques Road Show* plays in the living room. I think I'll take an early night, make an early start tomorrow.

But it's a bit of a worry, to be honest. The only think I have to look forward to tomorrow is making an application for JSA.

Chapter Five

A lot of people don't know that my father is black – Ryan Giggs

"Day saver, please," I say as cheerfully as possible to the bus driver, dropping the exact change into the little slot.

The bus to Bridgend comes every two hours. In London they wave their suitcases in frustration if the next tube doesn't come within five minutes.

I've never had a good relationship with bus drivers and, if truth be told, they scare me a bit. It has always been a mystery. I always politely ask for a bus ticket, smile, and I say please and thank you, just like my mum taught me. I've never turned up with a big note or a debit card and asked for cash back, which sometimes I'd like to do. This is the twenty-first century, after all. And yet, every time, they've looked at me as though I've said something absolutely *ridiculous*, like I've asked for a Big Mac with large fries or something. Surely, I think, asking for a bus ticket on a bus must be a reasonably common request?

This one is not too bad at all. He is a skinny guy with long, bony fingers. I don't fancy his prospects. Probably hasn't had a lay for quite some time. He nods his head and prints the ticket, no problems at all. I say thank you, and he makes some sort of noise, at least. This could be a good day, I think.

I haven't caught the bus since I was sixteen, when my exams were at funny times of the day. I'd get off the bus in town and meet Sam for something to eat before heading to the school to face the dreaded exams. If truth be told, I've never been the most naturally gifted academically, not like Sam, which might just be an academic way of saying that I'm not really all that bright, who knows? But that's not fair, not really. I can have a pretty intellectual conversation with somebody when I choose to and my vocabulary, for example, can be extensive. I just have problems *remembering* things that don't really interest me too much, which was always a problem when it came to exams, if I remember correctly. I've always managed to get there in the end – passed all my exams and all that – which is more than can be said for Den - but it was never easy. It involved what my dad would probably call 'graft' and what my mum would call 'stress.' Thinking about it now, it may be part of the reason why I always have a feeling of anxiety when I board a bus, because I remember those exams?

Anyhow, as the bus only comes every two hours, I'd sort of assumed it would at least be fairly full. Thinking back now though to those lonely journeys when I was sixteen, the bus was never very busy. Now, there are just two elderly ladies with shopping trolleys sat a couple of seats from the back. The back seats were always reserved for the cool kids in school, and still I feel a sense of hierarchy. I take a seat right in the middle of the bus and press my temple against the window and stare out at the passing countryside (of which there is plenty).

The women are talking. With three of us on the bus, it is impossible not to listen.

"So, Hilary, did you watch the *Graham Norton Show* last night?"

"No, Lynne, I was watching *Benidorm* on repeat."

"It had that little funny guy on it, you know, the one who looks like a hard boiled egg. Ever so funny he was, Hilary."

"Oh, I know the one. Got one of those funny faces, hasn't he? Just can't remember his name. It will come to me, though. Hold on, is it George Lucas?"

"No, George Lucas is the director, you know, the one who did *Star Wars.* Ever so clever, he is. Love his films. But that's not the one who was on *Graham Norton,* though."

"It's going to bother me all day now, Lynne, trying to think who it is. Wish I'd watched it now. Got *Benidorm* saved, I have."

My phone rings. The ring tone is *My Humps* by *Black Eyed Peas*. I'd spent quite a bit of time in the week choosing a decent one. It's quite possible that I was using this time as a distraction from looking for work. Katie's name appears on my phone. She has phoned me a few times and I've ignored her a few times, but now I don't have anything to do apart from listen to Hilary and Lynne work out who was on the *Graham Norton Show* last night, and it will probably be twenty minutes before we hit Bridgend. I click the answer button.

"Oh, hello," I say, all bright and cheerful, like a friendly dinner lady dishing out the mashed potatoes to little school children. *Nice young man*, Hilary and Lynne must be thinking. I turn to the window and in a much less cheerful tone I whisper "what's up, slag?"

There is a pause. Silence. Katie hisses, irritably. "Nick, don't be a child."

"It's great to talk to you," I say, loudly and enthusiastically, so that Hilary and Lynne can hear me. Then, quietly and less enthusiastically, "talk, bitch."

There is silence again. I can imagine her face on the end of the phone, scowling. God, I think, Katie really looks *sexy* when she is angry. I wonder what she is wearing. Wonder whether it would be an inappropriate time and place to initiate some…only my thoughts are interrupted…

"Nick, why have you run away back to…" she pauses now, as if preparing herself to utter a dirty word, "*Wales?*"

I'm angry now. She has hit a nerve. However much I moaned about the place to her when I was in London, it is still where I'm from and anyway, it's okay for me to bitch about it, not her. "Listen, Katie, I know that with your narrow-minded *The Only Way Is Essex* outlook on life, you think Wales is all about sheep and farmers, but this is where I am from, and besides, there is still plenty of opportunity in Wales nowadays…"

I may have gone over the top a bit here. The bus slows down to a virtual stop. Three sheep idly cross the road, without a care in the world. I've raised my voice. I wonder what on earth Hilary and Lynne think of me now. I needn't have worried. "Good man! You tell her!" one of them shouts from the back, probably swinging the shopping bag in the air.

"Listen, Katie," I shout into my phone, playing to my

audience now, “I know that you love me, but this obsession needs to end. I just cannot return your love. If you continue harassing me then I will have no choice but to involve the police. Thank you and goodbye.”

I press call end. I know that’s it. She will not contact me again. To be honest, she hasn’t exactly made much effort to contact me since that night anyway. And she was never contacting to try and sort things out, begging me to forgive her. Six months we were together and I wonder why we even bothered. I’m not sure how it makes me feel now, though. I know she is not good for me. It was good to have somebody, though, especially someone who looked that good. Now, there is nobody. And I’m back in a country that doesn’t feel like home anymore, like I don’t belong any more. It makes me feel a bit scared.

The rest of the journey is completed in silence. As I’m getting off the bus, I hear Lynne say, “I know who it was! It was Matt Lucas!”

“That’s the little bastard!” Hilary enthusiastically exclaims, as she struggles to get her shopping trolley off the bus.

I’ve got an age to kill. My signing time is 13:30. The 13:05 bus would get me in about five minute too late, and I’ve been reliably informed that I may as well chop my balls off if I’m even a minute late.

I stroll through the Rhiw Arcade. Nothing much seems to have changed, apart from the fact that people seem keener and more eager for your money. A man in a slick suit tries to convince me that I should claim compensation for buying PPI, even though I tell him I’m pretty damn sure I’ve never bought PPI before. Another man, with matching lopsided glasses and teeth, tries to convince me I cannot possibly live without breakdown cover as you ‘never know when disaster may strike,’ even though I don’t have a car and don’t drive. Both men shake their heads and pull a pained face when I say thanks, but no thanks. I can’t help but feel guilty. They probably don’t earn much.

The rest of the streets have changed though, even in the short time I’ve been away. Some of the chain stores have been replaced by pound stores, by charity shops. If you wanted to buy some decent clobber, you'd be way out of luck. And I can't spot a single sports shop, not that I'd really need one, but still. There are less people walking around than I remember. And you can tell that people don't have much money to spare, that everyone is counting the pennies. I tell myself that it is like this in every town nowadays, what with the out of town places and the internet, but it hits home harder here because it's my home town and I remember it differently.

I find shelter in a little café just opposite the Jobcentre. The waitress calls me 'darling' and 'sweetheart,' which I quite like. I buy a coffee, and then a second. Look at my watch. Still got an hour and seventeen minutes left. I gaze into space.

It has been a full working week (although, to be accurate, I have not been working) since I've been home. I guess you could say I've given myself a little career break. I am now officially 'in between jobs.' Whenever my mum has asked me what I've been up to, I've told her that I've been looking at making a few changes to my CV. Which is true; I have been looking to make a few changes to my CV, I just haven't made them. Instead, I've been discovering just how addictive daytime TV is. Every hour of every day has been dictated by the scheduling of chat shows, documentaries and quiz shows. And I've mainly watched them alone. Dad has been pottering around in the shed and Mum has been rushing to and from fitness classes. It hit me that there really must be more to life when I turned on the TV in the middle of the afternoon one day to an American soap actress uttering the words, "there really is no shame in experiencing erectile dysfunction, Sheriff."

I think I really would have gone round the bend if my dad hadn't been hanging round the house, too. Dad took early retirement what must be three years or so ago now and it's fair to say that he probably hasn't made the most of all the spare time. He shares his days evenly between moping around in the house and moping around in the shed. When I say that he took early retirement, I've never actually had much idea what work he did in the first place. I know that he worked for the council in Bridgend, but as a kid that always equated to 'boring office job.' He started at nine and finished at five, Monday to Friday. And I never, ever remember him taking a day off, just like the lady on the Streatham Common to London Bridge train, I guess. Oh, and he was also the Union Representative, which always seemed a bit odd to me, because he's such a meek man, with no bite to him at all. I wouldn't want him defending me, put it that way. The only time I've ever seen him speak up is when somebody has said something negative about my mum, and to be honest, she has such a sharp tongue that she can look after herself anyway.

My thoughts are interrupted by something at the window, and I jump up, startled. It is not something, but *someone*; and that someone's face is pressed against the glass, big bulging eyes glaring straight at me. We're getting lynched, I think, and I consider hiding underneath the table. I glance away, pretending I haven't noticed anything, but the face is still there. I look again. The fuzziness clears, and things start coming into focus. The lips are puckered, shaped like a kiss. The guy is black. Heck, I think, in Bridgend that can only mean one thing…

It's my old mate, Dennard Ray Jones.

I've always found it ironic that possibly the only Jamaican family in Bridgend had a Welsh surname, but Den always assured me that it's a pretty common name there, too.

I once looked it up on the internet, and apparently 97% of the population of Bridgend is white, and I'd estimate, from my last visit to the Princess of Wales hospital, that at least another 2% is Philippine. My point is, when a black guy gestures to you in a café right in the middle of Bridgend, there's a pretty good chance that it's my good mate Den.

It's been – what? - over a year or so since Den last came to visit me in London, and the texts had fizzled out since, and I'd wondered whether our friendship was going to as well. A couple of years or so ago that would have been unthinkable. We'd always been close as thieves, you see, the three of us - me, Dennard Jones and Sam Thornton. I guess there's a major crack now that Sam has disappeared off the face of the earth and possibly…no, I don't want to think that…but anyway when I last saw Den it was as if my life had moved on and his hadn't. Or that it had moved, but backwards. Fair enough, we went West and got drunk and partied and had a laugh and all that but I did wonder, even at the time, what it would have been like if there wasn't any drink to help us along.

It feels almost surreal now, too, as here we are in his manor – Bridgend – and not my manor – London.

Den looks happy to see me, though. He shakes my hand, and there are about four moves to the shake, followed by a back slap. The guy looks really good, too. He has always been tall, but in school he was just as lanky as me. Now he has added some major bulk. Bizarrely, he is wearing a tee sheet that is split right down the middle with the red and white of Wales on one side and the green and yellow of Jamaica on the other. It might possibly be the tightest tee shirt seen by either country, and it does well to show off his expanding muscles. His hair is cut shorter than I remember it, it's probably a grade three or something, and he has light stubble on his chin. His big white smile is exactly how I remember it, though.

"Geezer!" he exclaims, "look at you, hey!" Den has one of the thickest Welsh accents I've ever heard, which always makes me smile.

"Keep your money in your pocket, feller," he says, holding his palms out. "This is on me. Coffee, yeah?"

"White, two sugars, please, Den," I reply, and as the words come out of my mouth I realise that this will be my third coffee, and that my hands have already started shaking.

"I remember," he says. "You like your coffee white and your women black, yeah?"

He is not usually that loud, Den. He has deep nasal tones and is fairly quietly spoken. Sam was the excitable one.

I know he is referring, yet again, to the drunken snog I had in a kebab house about five years ago with one of the few black girls I've ever actually seen in Bridgend.

"I know how much you like your black girl, big man,"

Den says, as he leans across the counter and the waitress calls him 'sweetheart.'

He returns with two big mugs. "So what you doing here, then?" he asks. "I thought that you were Alan Sugar's apprentice in London?"

"I'm back now."

Den breaks into a laugh, and I'm confused why. What's so funny? He seems to have more teeth than I remember, and they seem whiter than humanly possible. The only guy I've ever seen with a bigger, whiter smile in all my days is Den's brother, Patrick.

"Picked up a bit of a London accent there, mate," he says. "I'm from Lon-don town, fancy buying some jellied eels?" he mimics, putting on a surprisingly decent cockney accent. It's strange. My mum has been babbling on about my accent all week, usually when I've said something that she doesn't agree with. "Oh, Nicholas," she's been saying, breaking into a laugh, "you and your London accent!"

Den leans back in the tattered chair and flexes his muscles. I tap a coin nervously against the plastic table. "So how you been, Nick? What you back for?"

I think about telling him that I was a big player in London, that I'm currently enduring a temporary blip in my plan for world domination; I'm always the same when I haven't seen somebody for a while, but I get the impression Den wouldn't be impressed by this kind of talk anyway. I think that was part of the problem when he last came to London. So I tell him the truth; that I found my best mate shagging my missus and I quit my job after I told my boss to go fuck himself.

It's just like Harry in the pub. He finds it hysterical. I wait for him to stop laughing. Eventually, when he does, he leans forward, ready to ask another question.

"So, what position were they doing it in, mate?"

"What the....?" I protest, my voice going all high-pitched. "What has that got to do with anything?"

Den is trying not to laugh again. "I'm just trying to picture the scene, geezer," he says, innocently enough. "Little details are all important, you know. The Mona Lisa is only the Mona

Lisa because of that crooked little smile, you know, and the Leaning Tower of Pisa wouldn't be the Leaning Tower of Pisa if it wasn't, well, leaning, like? So, was she bent over on all fours, mate? Or doing reverse cowgirl, maybe? Yee-hah, cowboy! I need to picture the scene, you know…"

I can tell that he is just on the wind up, and it hits me that I really don't mind. Banter has no limits amongst friends and, back on his manor, he feels much more like a friend again. It's making me laugh, too. "You always were a twat, Den," I say, honestly.

"So what you going to do now then, Nick?" he asks, changing the subject. I preferred it when he wasn't being serious.

"Looking for a job, I guess," I say. "That's why I'm here today. I've got to sign on later. Bit embarrassing, really. Hopefully it will be short lived, yeah? My dad says that with my experience and qualifications I won't be out of work for long."

I realise I sound like a bit of a twat now. I'm like the kid from the milk adverts I saw on that TV programme whose dad said that if he doesn't drink milk, he'll only be good enough to play for Accrington Stanley. I momentarily ponder whether the boy drunk his milk or whether he now leads the forward line, before reminding myself that it was only an advert, after all.

"So, how *is* Mr Charles Evans then?" Den asks with a smile. "Still pottering around in his shed?"

"Mr Charles Evans can't complain, no he can't complain," I say, sounding like Fred Elliot from *Corrie.* "And yes, he is still pottering around in his shed."

"Still watching all that porn, yeah? No wonder he lost most of his hair."

"He paints in there!" I protest, although I really have no idea what my dad does inside that green shed of his.

"And how about the lovely Mrs Deborah Evans?"

"She's fine."

"Yes," Den says, licking his lips. "She sure *is* fine. Does she still have a thing for Derek the weatherman?"

This may sound like a strange thing to ask, but in reality,

it is quite a reasonable question, because my mum has always had a thing for Derek the weatherman. She thinks he is adorable. Whenever he comes on the TV, she is like 'oh look, its Derek the weatherman,' as if he doesn't normally present the weather on the same channel and at the same time every night. I'm sure that in her wildest daydreams, they go for long coastline walks together like on his programmes, the wind blowing through their hair. I quickly delete the thought from my mind. I really don't want to think about my mother's wildest daydreams.

"My mother doesn't have a thing for Derek," I say, unconvincingly. "She just thinks that he has a real nice screen presence, that's all. And she finds his walking programmes informative and helpful."

"Whatever," Den says dismissively. "When I was at your house it was always Derek this and Derek that. I'm sure she had a Derek calendar up on the fridge. One month he had his top off in front of a rainbow, the next month he had his trousers down in a thunderstorm..."

I laugh at this, despite myself. Den always had a way of taking things to extremes.

A girl eating a baguette walks past the window. She catches Den's eye and smiles.

"Now, *there's* a girl who looks right at home with a footlong in her mouth," Den comments, matter-of-factly.

All the time we talk, people walking past wave and knock on the window at my old mate, both men and women. This is definitely his manor.

"So, what you been up to then, Den?" I ask.

I'd been a bit reluctant to ask this. Last time I'd seen him, he had been unemployed for God knows how long and not really heading anywhere in particular. The guy had always had a majorly relaxed way about him, but in school he still wanted to do well and he worked hard at his exams. I wasn't seeing any of that determination or drive now.

His eyes flitter from side to side. He looks a bit vulnerable, and it's strange to see, for he's such a big, confident guy. "I guess it's been quite a time for me recently," he says, and he punches his big barrel chest as if to emphasise the point. "I've needed to ask myself some deep questions, what I really want from life, be honest with myself, you know, now that I've just come out..."

Wow, I think. I try to be as sensitive and as non-judgmental as possible. I think about that course I went on. "That's great, mate," I say. "It must have been a very big thing. I mean, as children, I always had my suspicions, but it never mattered, not one bit. And I guess when Gareth Thomas came out, it made a statement. If the Welsh rugby captain is comfortable with his sexuality, then we all should be."

Den screws his face up. He still has a light layer of freckles on his cheeks, and they disappear now. I wonder whether I have gone over the top with my sensitivity. Then the light switch goes on. "Not out of the closet! Out of prison! I been doing time, haven't I?" he says.

I feel a bit stupid, so I quickly try to change the subject. "Oh, sorry, mate. What you do…?"

"Anyway, what you mean you had your suspicions?" he interrupts. The guy looks a bit put out, to be honest.

"Oh, I was only kidding, big man," I say, unconvincingly. "So what were you inside for?"

This isn't the first time that Den has been inside, mainly for petty offences, but they all add up, I guess, and so by now I imagine that his card has been marked.

Den looks a bit embarrassed now. The spark has dimmed. "Got caught up in the riots, didn't I?"

"Caught up…?"

"Yeah, you know? I got caught up in the flow of things. Stole a flat screen from Dixons, didn't I?"

"Which Dixons?"

"The one down the road."

"But there weren't any riots in Bridgend?"

"Okay, so I guess I wasn't part of the official riots themselves, but it was at the same time that the riots were going on, you know. And I guess I am quite a well known figure around here nowadays. The judge thought that I was trying to lead something. I think he thought I had real leadership qualities, you know. But really I just wanted to give a new flat screen to my mum, like. He made an example of me. I was a victim of being in the wrong place at the wrong time," he says.

A victim who just happened to be running away from the scene of a crime with a flat screen television under his arm, I think, but I keep that to myself. It does explain why the texts had completely vanished over the last few months, though.

"Oh right." I change the subject again. "So how is your mum, then? And Patrick?"

Den has always been close to his mum, a bubbly, attractive full-bodied woman who would make Vin Diesel run for safety. "Yeah, my mum is good; still the same, you know?" His eyes divert away from me now. "And Patrick, he's the same too, I guess. Ducking and diving, getting into trouble, you know how it is."

I pause and take a deep breath.

"And, have you heard from…?"

Den knows exactly what I am asking, and he lowers his eyes and shakes his head slowly from side to side. I know what his answer will be before I've even asked the question. I have to ask though, just in case. "Not a thing from Sam, mate. They think it was probably suicide, you know? He's been missing for that long now, and there have been no traces of anyone seeing him in the local area for that long, now."

It hurts, real bad, to actually hear somebody - somebody close- utter these dreaded words, but in reality he's only saying what I've secretly been thinking for years. And it is a rational conclusion to reach, what with the sudden disappearance, and in this area, too.

"I keep getting those dreams," I tell Den.

He feigns a smile. "What, the one in the swimming pool where you forget your trunks and everyone is laughing?"

"No," I say quickly. "I only had that dream once!" I can't even remember telling Den about that one, but I guess I must have. Mind you, I remember telling Sam about it back in school, and he always did have a big mouth. Maybe he told him? "You know, the one where the three of us meet up and he seems really well and then he just disappears again."

Den takes a long slurp of his coffee and nods his head. He knows exactly what dream I'm talking about, and I can see he's considering this one carefully. "It is a tough one, Nick. We all respond to these things in different ways. There will always be a place for Sam in my heart, you know? He will always be a part of my life. But I guess I've just accepted that it will only be in the heart, yeah. I think that you know that, too, but I guess you can never be in control of your dreams, can you?"

I know he is right. Den nearly always talks sense. He just tends to do the opposite of whatever he says. The most appropriate words I've ever heard him say were 'do as I say, and not as I do.' I raise my mug and click it against his and I say thanks for being a good mate. Right now it feels strange that we haven't seen each other for so long.

"So what time you signing on, feller?"

"Half one."

"Just remember to repeat over and over, with real passion in your heart man, that you *really* want a job. 'I *want* to work!' is the favourite catchphrase in there, especially with those who will do anything to get out of working. It makes for an easier life, yeah?"

I nod my head appreciatively and reach into my pocket and pull out my signing book. Something catches Den's eye and he grabs hold of my card.

"This is R week."

I don't say anything, but I am sure my face is saying *what you on about?*

"This week is P week, you bozo," he says. "You're signing next Friday, not today!"

I should be pissed, I know I should. My whole morning has revolved around this signing. And yet, I don't feel pissed at all. It just doesn't seem to matter, now that I've met up with Den again.

We are out in the street. The wind has died down, but it is getting colder. It's raining, and puddles are already forming on the pavement. He says he'll text me, arrange to meet up. Just like the old days, he says. I shake his hand. There are five moves to his handshake this time.

As I wait for the bus, I wonder whether Lynne and Hilary have finished their shopping yet.

Chapter Six

I warn you not to be ordinary, I warn you not to be young, I warn you not to fall ill, and I warn you not to grow old – Neil Kinnock

It is one heck of a long street. If you stand at one end and squint, then you can just about make out the last house on the other end of the street, but only just. The terraced houses all look the same, except for an occasional hanging basket or a sticker saying beware, we own a lethal dog.

I knock on a green door number eight. The glass is glazed and I can just about make out a shape edging slowly towards me, and not in any great hurry either, or so it seems. The lady eyes me suspiciously, like I'm going to try and sell her double glazing, or maybe eternal salvation. The lady looks very glamorous, especially considering it's only eleven o'clock on Saturday morning. She wears a long white summer dress which flows all the way to her ankles, sparkling earrings dangle from her ears, and she proudly displays perfectly manicured purple nails.

"Hello, Nanny Joyce," I say, kissing her on the cheek and inhaling the strong perfume that she always wears.

"Ah, Nick," she says, hugging me. She feels bony and angular in my arms, all sharp edges. "Come in. Now this *is* a nice a surprise. It's my favourite grandson. Make yourself at home."

Nanny Joyce has always referred to me as her favourite grandson, even though I'm her only grandson. She guides me down the narrow hallway to the lounge. My body almost disintegrates into the soft, worn sofa. I'm sure that the springs went back in the eighties.

Without asking whether or not I want a drink, she departs to the kitchen and starts boiling water in a pan. There is a strong smell of soap. She has been washing clothes by hand, in the sink. A book, the history of the TUC between 1866 and

1966, has been left open on the sofa. I wonder if it is a riveting read.

"It's truly wonderful that you're back in Bridgend, Nick. That London is such a crowded, dirty place. I tell you, even the trees look dirty in London!" she exclaims before pursing her lips and taking a sip of tea.

"I needed that," she says, even though my nan is well known for drinking up to ten cups of tea a day. Oh, not to mention the twenty or so fags. When anyone comments on this, she will happily just reply something along the lines of, "I'm eighty-one now, I've lived long enough. If I'm going to go, I may as well go smoking a cigarette."

She looks at me now and her eyes narrow. A couple of frowns appear on the side of her cheeks. She has remarkably good skin for someone her age.

"A little bird tells me that you are still unemployed and living off taxpayers money, Nick," my nan casually says. I know that this 'little bird' is my dad; her son-in-law. The cup in her hand is shaking slightly. She has a tremor now following the minor stroke that she had last year. Sometimes there is a slur to her voice, but otherwise it does not seem to have affected her much. She goes back to the kitchen and returns with a plate of biscuits, digestives because "I know you like dipping them in your tea."

"It's only a short term blip until I find suitable employment, Nan," I reply, making sure that my biscuit does not completely dissolve in the tea and sink to the bottom of the cup.

"Well don't be looking for too long, Nick. Your mother and father are worried sick about you. And you know, you have the best parents in the whole of South Wales, you really don't know how lucky you are, I tell you. When I was a little girl, I woke up one Christmas and do you know what I found in my stocking…?"

"An apple and an orange?"

"Yes," Nan says with a grin, stabbing a finger at me. "Just an apple and an orange, I tell you. And the orange was bruised too, half of it was black. But your grandfather, Albert and I, God bless his soul, we tried to do the best we could for your mother, and your parents have done exactly the same for you, Nicholas."

I nod my head. I know that my parents have been very good. I have been very lucky. It just doesn't always feel that way.

She stares at me now, like she has lost her train of thought. "Anyway, what were you saying, Nick?" she asks.

"Just that I'm still temporarily in between employment, Nan," I say, rather loudly, but I'm not sure why, because my Nan has perfect hearing.

"Oh, yes," she says, eyes flicking to the ceiling, as if she is trying to remember me saying this.

"Maybe take something temporary, yes? Temporary jobs can quickly turn into permanent careers," my eighty-one-year-old grandmother says. It seems very familiar, and then I realise she sounds like my mum.

"It would be nice to find some job security," I say, hoping this will impress her, as Nan is usually very keen on job security.

"Well with the current climate, Nick," she says, holding the cup and swishing the tea around in a circle, as if looking for some answers, "a job is a job. Mrs Singleton's grandson, Jason, used to be a manager for a confectionery company. He was quite high up, too; he could take home all the sweets he wanted, the lucky bleeder. It was the perfect job. He was actually quite a fat man, so I've been told. Anyway, they only went and made him redundant, didn't they? The buggers. He's been looking for a job for eighteen months Nick, and he's as thin as a stick of pepperoni now. So be thankful for small mercies, I say."

"I could do with losing a bit of weight, Nan," I say, pushing out my little belly and patting it with my hand.

"Cheeky bugger," she says, laughing.

I reach out for one of the newspapers, which are folded carefully on the table next to the sofa. They've been passed down by the famous Mrs Singleton, grandmother of the now stick thin Jason, who lives next door. I'm sure that if I looked in the Guinness Book of Records it would confirm that Mrs Singleton is in fact the oldest person in Wales. Nan has known her for over fifty years, and yet she has always been Mrs Singleton and not Barbara or Pat or whatever her first name may be. Mrs Singleton comes over every morning at nine o'clock, after she has finished reading the papers herself, and gives them to Nan. It is always the Telegraph, because it is the best read, and the Sun, because it has the best crossword and which, I notice, has already been completed by Nan.

"Is your mum okay?" Nan asks, and she scratches at the arm on her chair, as if she has noticed a stain. "Is she well?"

I assure Nan that she is, and she smiles. All her teeth are white apart from one, which looks yellow, probably stained through years of smoking. I'm sure, though, that she has invested in a teeth whitening product at some point.

"A little bird told me that you're back in contact with your friend from school, that young Den," my Nan says, dipping a biscuit in her tea.

The little bird seems to tell her a hell of a lot, especially considering whenever I come here with him, he sits and reads the paper or goes out the back and mows the lawn. My nan is the only person I know who asks my dad how his painting is going, rather than whether he is still pottering around in the shed. It's always been a joke that you're not supposed to like your mother-in-law, but that sure doesn't seem to be the case with my dad.

"That Dennard always was a handsome little devil, all that brown chocolate skin," she says. "I tell you, Nick, if I was fifty years younger…"

I've heard my nan say this fifty years younger thing before, about various men, including Jamie Oliver. "He certainly knows his way around the kitchen," she said once when we were watching one of his cookery programmes. "I tell you, Nick, if I was fifty years younger…"

"Fifty years is a bit optimistic isn't it Nan?" I ask now. "I thought you said you flew a spitfire during the Second World War?"

"Why, you cheeky…" but she never finishes her sentence.

"What about your other friend, is it Sam? Now, he really

was a pretty boy. He had eyelashes that even I was jealous of, and I used to be a real looker in my day, let me tell you. Such a lovely nature, that boy, too. Ever so thoughtful. And he could talk for Wales, you know, but he listened, too. I always thought that he would make a great nurse or a doctor."

I'm a little taken aback by this. My nan knows that Sam went missing, and so she never asks about him.

"We still can't find him," I say, and I see now that something seems to click in Nan's mind and then she says "oh yes, of course, he went missing, of course he did. Sorry, dear."

Nanny Joyce has lived by herself for as long as I can remember. She married my granddad, Albert, my mum's dad, when she was eighteen. There is a black and white wedding photo of them on the sideboard, where Nan looks like a movie star, with her long flowing hair and perfect porcelain skin, smiling glamorously at the camera. Granddad Albert, on the other hand, has a big shiny head and wears a heavy, bulky suit, and he looks about one hundred and sixty, even then. There is another one of him on the beach, and he is wearing a suit then, too. Albert had a stroke in 1979 and my nan looked after him until he died about seven years later. I can't remember him, of course, but my Mum says that he was the kindest man she ever knew, the last of the true gentlemen.

My nan goes in her handbag and pulls out a yellow packet of Lockets. She knows that they are my favourite, and she always has a healthy supply of them hidden away somewhere. "I got you these," she says, "but remember, eat one at a time. They're not sweets, you know."

I gratefully take the packet and run upstairs to the toilet, slipping two into my mouth on the way. Trevor, Nan's black cat, sits lazily in a ball by the toilet door. He sees me and then reluctantly stretches his legs out and moves out of the way. The look he gives me, however, suggests that he is far from happy about it. My nan has had Trevor for what must be ten years now, even though she is adamant she is allergic to cats. I once asked her why she named a cat Trevor and not something like, I don't know, Fluffy or Tom or whatever cats are usually called. Nan informed me that he was named after Trevor Sinclair, the QPR footballer. When I asked her why, she said "he's black, isn't he?" To this day, I'm still not sure whether it was a politically correct thing to do.

There is a metal frame around the toilet that wasn't there the last time. I guess my nan must be struggling with her balance but then, she seems okay on her feet to me. Back downstairs, we chat about the latest books that we have read – my Nan has just finished *The Luck of the Tories*, about Neil Kinnock, and *Being Jordan* by, well, Jordan. After an hour, I ask her whether she has any lunch for me, and she tells me that she has already given me lunch, and nods at the biscuits. I was only joking, of course. I wouldn't dare eat any of the food that my nan cooks.

At the door, Nan wishes me the best of luck with my job search and asks me to give my love to my mum and dad. I kiss her on the cheek and again inhale the scent of her strong perfume.

It is a short walk to the train station. My feet are busy avoiding the cigarette butts and the cracks in the pavement, just for fun.

My mind, however, is once again busy wondering why my mum and my nan have not spoken to each other for all the years that I can remember.

Chapter Seven

I like to drink to suit my location – Tom Jones

"Geezer," I say, pausing to take two full gulps of lager. "The passing of the years has made your memory fuzzy. You'll be talking about spaceships and aliens next. Sam and I were in on it all along. You were never very subtle, big man, especially after ten cans of *Tennent's Extra*."

"Whatever," Den retorts. "You made Casper look like he'd just come back from a two week holiday in Majorca that night. Although, fair play, I guess that you are one pasty white guy, anyway, like."

Its ten o'clock and the two of us are out in Bridgend, 'living it large'. The Oak on Adare Street is filling up nicely. Most of the punters are regulars and some look like they've been sitting on their bar stools since the war, but it is kind of good to feel like a youngster again.

I was waiting out the back in the beer garden when Den arrived, some three hours or so earlier.

"That's what I like to see," Den had said, reaching out for my hand, and I was by now getting used to his shakes. "My old school mate in a beer garden with just a cold one for company. Put those hands back in your pocket, geezer; the next one is on me. Why you looking so smart, anyway, Jamie Redknapp?"

I told him that I'd been for an interview in Cardiff earlier in the day. It was just for a Senior Executive Officer at *Lombard and Morgan.* I would have been taking a serious pay cut from my last job, but I'm getting used to the fact now that there are London wages and then the rest of the world wages. Anyway, it is all irrelevant now, as I won't get the job.

"I spent the first half of the interview telling them in great detail how fantastic I was," I explained to Den as the first cold, refreshing lager was just beginning to take effect, "and then I spent the second part of the interview back-tracking. They wanted to know why, if I was so incredibly wonderful, I was willing to take a cut in pay and responsibility to work for their lowly company in Cardiff. It had me a bit stumped, to be honest, Den."

Den told me that acting smart did not suit me, and besides, acting at a lower intellectual level is a better approach because expectations are set lower and when they are surpassed, people are suitably impressed. I tried protesting that acting dumb in an interview may not have been the best approach, but he was dismissive, waving his hand at me and sending me to the bar.

And it continued from there. The banter was fast and the drinking was faster. There was never any suggestion the conversation might turn serious and it felt great. It mattered not one bit that I was still unemployed, that I had nobody in my life and no clue even where my life was heading. My old friend was in exactly the same boat as me, and it had been a long time since that was the case. We were living for the moment. Right now, right here, we were out, living it large and drinking lager. Just the two of us. I wished that it was three, but nothing else mattered. Nothing else was real. Not for now, anyway.

"So where did all this muscle come from?" I ask Den, pinching an exposed bicep. "When I first met you, you reminded me of a runner bean."

"Runner beans are green," Den retorted, as though this was the only obvious difference between him and a runner bean. "I train hard," he says, taking a long swig of his lager and then a mouthful of dry roasted peanuts. "I follow a carefully planned exercise routine that contains a measured balance between cardiovascular and free weights. And my diet has a heavy protein emphasis, minimising carbohydrates and unhealthy fats."

"Oh yes, those dreaded carbohydrates," I say, realising that I must be getting drunk as I can hardly even say the word. I start laughing, then realise that Den isn't. I raise my eyebrows and lean forward, waiting for the punch line. None comes. "No shit?" I say.

"You don't just fall out of bed in the morning looking this good," Den replies, clenching his arm and giving his bicep a kiss. "It takes work. And the ladies are there to pick up the benefits of all that hard graft, let me tell you," and he laughs wickedly.

I'm at the bar again. I try to count how many I've had, but give up after eight. The barmaid, who I noticed earlier had a large forehead and a receding hairline, now has glowing, flawless skin and a cute little gap between her front two teeth. I innocently smile at her, but she pulls a face and serves the guy next to me, who I swear has only just joined the queue. I guess they haven't seen a man in a decent suit round these parts before. Fair play to the guy, he points in my direction signalling that I was next. The barmaid doesn't even glance at me. *It's alright, butt*, she says to the guy. *What can I get you?*

We finish the drink quick time and head to a club. The bouncers eye me suspiciously, even though I swear that I look no different from any other punter entering the establishment, as I'm all blurry-eyed and unsteady on my feet. Lo and behold, surprise surprise, Den knows the bouncers and there are back-slaps and elaborate handshakes all round. We go straight to the front of the queue (admittedly, there are only five others waiting, but it feels good, regardless).

I haven't been to this club for about three years but, as we climb the thick carpeted stairs, the whole aroma of the place feels instantly familiar. A strong smell of stale beer and sweaty feet wafts through the air. It has nothing on the swanky bars in London, but all the same, I can't wait to get to the top of the stairs and get involved in the action of the club. I notice my blurred reflection in a mirror. My cheeks looks flushed and my eyes red. What surprises me most, though, is the big smile on my face. I almost don't recognise myself.

"Bloody hell, it's like being in a *wonga.com* advert in here," Den guffaws in my ear.

It isn't busy yet. There are a few people spread out on the tattered sofas and there is a group of men on the slot machines. Den goes to the bar and I take a seat. The banter continues and I can hear it but I'm not really listening. I'm looking around, big cheesy grin filling my cheeks. Time passes without me saying anything. It feels like a dream. I want to touch people's faces, check that they are really there. The lager tastes so sweet. I take a sip and then another. My lips feel glued to the glass, addicted to the taste.

I notice that Den has gone over to speak to some ladies on the next sofa. He reminds me of a wolf looking to eat some sheep. I sense Den coming back to the table, somewhere, next to me.

"Good news, Casanova," he says, prodding me on the shoulder. I think I need sunglasses; the glare from his teeth is so bright. "I just informed some fine ladies that my good friend over here is newly single and highly eligible and is searching for no-strings fun; and the one on the end wants to speak to you."

I wonder when I told Den that I was looking for no-strings fun, but my thoughts seem muddled up, the words in my mind all back-to-front. I glance over and, sure enough, the girl on the end giggles and gives me a wave. I say 'girl,' but even in this light and with the beer goggles that I just know I'm wearing, I can see that she is most definitely a lady of advancing years. Who cares? My standards have already been lowered just by being in this place, so I may as well push it to the limits. I'm straight on my feet, like a dog on heat.

"Ask her about her right hand, Nicholas," Den shouts to my back. "She mentioned that she shook Donny Osmond's hand at the concert in Birmingham and she hasn't washed it since. It may be a good conversation starter, what you think?"

I turn and look at my friend who looks so handsome and clever and glowing right now and I pat him on the shoulder. "Cheers mate," I say.

The woman makes room for me next to her. She is wearing black flared trousers and she has a little pot belly that is straining the fabric. She is a size sixteen in a size fourteen top. Her face is caked in make-up and there are quite a few cracks. She has long black eyelashes that she flutters seductively at me. Her perfume smells good, all feminine and flowery.

"What's your name then, pretty lady?" I ask, smiling, and just for a moment, she has two heads.

"Mandy," she says, and she smiles, too. I notice that her teeth look good, fresh and white, but one of them is heading in a slightly different direction from the others.

"So, Mandy, are you having a good night?"

"I am now," she says, and puts her hand on my leg.

I remember what Den said and thought that I'd impress her with my insight and knowledge.

"So what's this I hear about you shaking Donny's hand?" I ask, taking the said hand and theatrically kissing it, like a prince kissing his princess.

She giggles all coyly now. "Is that what he said? Well, young man, that's not quite right."

"So what happened then, Mandy?" I ask, kissing her hand again.

"Well, I did meet Donny, but I didn't shake his hand. No, I wanked him off backstage…"

I drop the hand immediately. Mandy gives me *oh and aren't I a bad girl* look.

And then, I just can't stop laughing.

I turn around and Den isn't there. I kiss Mandy on the cheek and say thank you. She looks happy enough. I'm sure I hear her shouting to me that she was only joking, that she didn't really do anything with poor Donny, but it doesn't really matter. I go looking for Den. He is on the dance floor. I'm right out there in the thick of it with him. The DJ is playing *Someone Like You.* I close my eyes, swing my hips and think that I may still be unemployed and have nobody in my life and no clue where my life is heading, but *this is the life,* right here, right now.

Chapter Eight

Diamonds never leave you – men do! – Shirley Bassey

Tuesday afternoon between one-thirty and three is Pilates for my mother in the village hall. Wednesday from two is yoga, and Friday at three is her ladies meeting. And as today is Tuesday, it is Pilates at one-thirty.

"Please don't forget," Mum said, blue mat rolled up under her arm, a kiss planted on my stubbly cheek, "to pick me up from the pub at four-thirty, Nick."

There was no way that I could forget. She'd reminded me a zillion times that morning.

"Your father always picks me up from the pub at four-thirty on Tuesdays, Nicholas," my mother had begun, two days earlier. "I think it would be nice if you could pick me up instead. It will give your father a rest for a change. He deserves that, don't you think, Nick?"

I glanced at my father, who was sat in his usual chair, and I noticed that his hair was sticking up one side, which was unusual as his hair was usually immaculately pressed down, as though he ironed it. His back was regimentally straight and his feet were flat against the floor. I was amazed by how very little he seemed to be doing. He was not even watching the TV or cleaning his nails. The best – and I mean the *very* best – you could say was that he was staring absent-mindedly into space.

"Yes," I replied, trying to hide sarcasm from my voice. "I guess he does deserve the rest, mum, he looks all worn out."

Now, Tuesday afternoon at four-thirty, and my mum is sitting outside the pub on a long wooden bench with the girls from Pilates. My feet sink into the freshly cut grass as I carefully shut the iron-clad gate behind me. The long stretch of lawn is bordered by a brick wall that must be all of eight feet tall. I'm suddenly aware that ten middle-aged ladies in tracksuit bottoms and (most probably) sports bras are staring straight at me. My mum is right in the thick of the group. She waves an enthusiastic hand at me.

"Oh, here he is, ladies," my mum coos, "my son, Nicholas."

A warm chorus of, "hi, Nicholas" follows.

I limply wave my hand and feel my cheeks redden.

"Come sit down next to me, Nick," one of the ladies says, seductively patting the space that she has just made especially for me.

"Oh, you can see where he gets his good looks from, can't you girls?" the woman says as I sit down. The ladies nod their heads and my mum glistens with pride.

"Yes," the woman continues. "Your Charles has always been a handsome man, Debbie."

The woman looks at me again and I can feel her appraising me.

"If I was twenty years younger, Debbie, I tell you…"

"So how was Pilates, ladies?" I interrupt.

"An absolute killer," a woman from the adjacent table replies, and the ladies laugh. I notice that the lady has a sagging chin which reminds me of a lizard. She looks older than the rest of the group, like she is maybe seventy or so.

"You know Mrs Jones, Nicholas," my mum dutifully informs me. "She is the aunty of Simon Williams' friend Christopher, from school. Remember?"

I'm thinking that I can't even remember who Simon Williams is, let alone his friend Christopher, which means that I sure as hell don't know his aunty. Mrs Jones is drinking a full pint of lager. We look at each other and smile. There is a definite connection; it's apparent that she doesn't have a clue who I am, either.

"Please, call me Sue," Mrs Jones says. "Yes, it was a killer, Nick. The young instructor, David, had us stretching in ways I'd never been stretched before."

"Speak for yourself, Sue," one of the ladies snorts.

"You know who David is," my mother interjects. "He is the grandson of Mrs Thomas, the cook from school."

I remember Mrs Thomas alright. She stood in the kitchen slapping a big wooden spoon against the palm of her hand, staring the young pupils down, daring them to scrape any uneaten food into the blue plastic bucket, which was apparently sent to Mr Evans' farm (next to our house) to feed the pigs. I was terrified of those pigs, because my mum had once told me that a young boy in Scotland had been eaten by one. Anyway, Mrs Thomas was the reason that I was always a chubby kid in Junior School. I only became lanky when I hit the big boys' school. But there again, I really don't have a clue who David, her grandson and the young man who has now stretched Mrs Jones in ways that she has never been stretched before, is.

One of the ladies returns from inside the pub with a tray full of drinks. It is a careful balancing act. "I took the liberty of buying you a pint of lager, Nick," the lady announces, placing it down in front of me. "You look like a lager drinker," she says, patting my shoulder with her hand.

"Thank you," I say. "I really appreciate that." I really did, too. I was gasping for a pint, but didn't much fancy going inside the pub, as the old black Labrador dog, Jesse, that lives there has always had a tendency to shag my leg.

"It was very nice of you to meet your mum after the pub," a lady says, raising her glass in my direction.

"I didn't really have much choice," I say, shrugging my shoulders, and they laugh.

"He's such a good boy, really," my mum says, sipping her drink. She doesn't usually praise me so highly. Her eyelids look heavy and I wonder whether or not this is her first drink, and then I further wonder whether her Tuesday afternoon Pilates classes are actually all that beneficial for her health.

"All he needs now is a job," she sighs, returning to normal.

It's time to change the subject. *How are you ladies finding the menopause?* I think of asking.

"Are any of you ladies fans of Donny Osmond, then?" I ask.

There is silence. Agonising moments pass. Then the lady with the snort, snorts, and then the rest of the group starts laughing, too.

“Cheeky bastard,” Mrs Jones, the seventy year old with the lizard neck, says. “Just how old do you think we are?”

“You can bring this one back again, Debbie,” another lady laughs.

The walk back to the house is a slow one. Mr Evans, the farmer with the pigs, passes in his battered old car at a real snail’s pace.

“I think Dai Evans thinks he is still driving his tractor,” my mum observes.

She thanks me when we get inside, and I can tell she means it. My dad is nowhere to be seen. He is most likely pottering around in the shed.

Chapter Nine

I spent many years laughing at Harry Secombe's singing until somebody told me it wasn't a joke – Spike Milligan

I'm an exceptional individual, devoted to progress and development.

It's official now; it says so on the first line of my CV.

Castle Street seems like a good place to start. There are plenty of recruitment agencies down there.

I'm not quite sure exactly what I'm expecting, but it definitely includes warm handshakes and wide, smug smiles. Walking into the first agency, however, nobody seems to be smiling. All of the desks are occupied, both with people and reams of paper. The phones are ringing off the hook, but everyone is already on one. Fans are blaring at level two, threatening to spill the paper and documents onto the blue carpeted floor. I stand in the entrance, beaming my best, professional smile, holding onto my wallet of CVs like it is the golden ticket from *Charlie and the Chocolate Factory*.

There is a young lad in front of me, talking to one of the consultants. He looks like he is straight out of school, and more recently, straight out of bed. His jeans are fashionably low, and his boxers are visible underneath. Oily spiky hair stands up at the top and on one side. His stature is best described as 'slumped'.

"What work are you looking for?" the woman asks.

"Anything, really; I'll really do absolutely anything at all, you know."

"Something in an office, maybe?"

"Oh, no. Don't think I could cope being inside all day. Anything else though."

"Door to door sales maybe?" the woman suggests.

"Fu- sorry, I mean, no, I don't think that would suit me, being outside and on my feet all day. I have sensitive skin."

"So you will do anything at all so long as its not indoors or outdoors then?" the lady asks, testily.

"Yes, that's right. I'll do absolutely anything apart from those two things."

"Okay, well we will keep hold of your CV and call you if anything comes up."

I shake my head from side to side as the lad trundles out of the door and I try to build some rapport with the consultant. My opening gambit is almost *youngsters these days hey,* but I have a last second rethink. She is probably in her early forties, I think, but it's quite difficult to tell because her foundation is so thick that it could hide a whole multitude of sins. It is quite difficult to read the look that she gives me, too, as it is possibly quite ambiguous, but no, I'm quite sure the look says *and what do you want?*

"How can I help?" she politely asks.

"I'm looking to register as a candidate for work with your well-established agency," I say, enthusiastically.

"We've only been open six weeks."

"Oh," I say, thinking fast. "But already making great strides, I hear."

"Not really. What work are you looking for?"

"Any executive position that would utilise my great array of experience and knowledge, really," I reply, confidently.

She doesn't look impressed. One of the girls on the phone looks up, and I don't think that she is either. "Can I have a look at your CV, please?" the consultant asks.

I carefully remove a single copy from the wallet and hand it to her. Her eyes quickly scan down the document.

"We have a sales job going at *Carphone Warehouse*," she says. "But I think you'll be over-qualified, to be honest with you. Worth a go, though?"

"*Carphone Warehouse*?"

"Yes, *Carphone Warehouse*," she says, without pausing. "They sell phones…"

"I know that," I interrupt, trying to keep my voice controlled. "I just don't really think it's for me."

The woman sort of shrugs her shoulders and I sort of shrug my shoulders back, and then there is an awkward moment when we both sort of shrug our shoulders at the same time, before I walk out.

I try four more agencies, and all in vain. The reactions vary, but they all have one thing in common – they are all distinctly negative. One agent literally laughs when I inform her of my salary expectations. I think she thinks I'm joking, but I'm not. *This is not London,* she says, shaking her head in disdain.

I sit on a bench facing Cardiff Castle, sipping a cup of tea. My legs ache. My head feels light. I check my watch again. Ten past two. It's probably time to go home, I think, or at least do some shopping.

Try one more, I tell myself. *You're a soldier,* I remind myself, a little weakly. And if that one's no good, I will treat myself to an ice cream.

It's a relief that at least there's air conditioning in this one. It's quieter, too. Probably the time of day, I think. Two desks are occupied, but they are both on the phone, as usual. I stand in the entrance, again. I think about walking out.

A girl comes from the back. She has black high heels and a skirt that comes down to her knees.

"What can I do for you, love?" she asks. Her red lips crease into a smile.

"I'm looking for a job."

"That's what we're here for," she laughs. It is a throaty cackle which suggests quite a serious smoking habit. "Could I have a look at your CV, then?"

I pull it out of the folder, not really caring whether it tears or not. I *hate* the thing. I'm ready with smart remarks this time. Burn it for all I care. She looks over it. No more than two pages, as all the websites said.

"Very impressive," she concludes.

"Very impressive?"

"Very impressive," she repeats. "Come and have a seat with me, pet."

This is the first time that I've been offered a seat all day. It's actually quite a comfortable one, as it turns out. I sit on her side of the desk, with a view of the screen. It's a blue swivel seat with wheels. I roll back and forth, making the most of the opportunity while it's there.

"So, are you a Nick or a Nicholas?" she asks. There are a few delicate lines around her mouth. She is probably early thirties, but I know I'm not good at guessing ages, as my previous encounters in nightclubs have only confirmed. She smells nice, like she dabs herself in perfume every hour, on the hour. There is a gap between the top two buttons of her cream blouse, and I glimpse a pink bra, probably from *Dorothy Perkins,* or somewhere.

"Well, only my mother calls me Nicholas when I've been naughty."

She laughs. "Well, I'll call you Nick then, and if you do something wrong, you'll know, because I'll call you Nicholas."

"Yes, mum," I say.

She laughs again, that deep throaty cackle. "And I'm Cath."

"Can I be honest with you, Nick?" she asks, swivelling in her chair to face me.

"Honest?" I say. "And you are really a Recruitment Consultant, yes?"

"Ha," she says, eyeing my CV again. "Nicholas, your personal statement says that you are, and I quote 'an exceptional individual, able to communicate at all levels, comfortable adapting my style to the individual circumstances. I am committed to development and progress, and accept nothing less than perfection in everything that I do.'"

She looks at me over the top of her glasses. Her eyes are blue but there are flecks of grey and green in with the mix, just for good measure. "Don't you think, Nick, that it makes you sound like a bit of a, well, to put it politely, a bit of a *dick,* no?"

Wow, I think. I wasn't really expecting *that.* I know she said she was going to be honest, but I thought that meant telling me that I had made a spelling mistake or something. "Well," I say, "that wasn't exactly the response that I was looking for."

Cath laughs again. Her and Den would be well suited. They would just laugh all day long. "I appreciate that," she interjects. "But better me saying that now than an employer reading through your personal statement and writing in big red letters all the way across it 'DICK,' right?"

There isn't much I can say to that. It definitely isn't the ideal scenario, for sure.

"And if I can shoot straight from the hip," she continues, " we don't really have any of these super executive jobs that you are looking for," and she points to the part on the page where it says, not in so many words, that I'm looking for a super executive job.

"Oh, right," I say, wondering why she asked me to take a seat in the first place.

"But Nick," she continues, "we could probably get you into a nice cosy temporary office job almost straight away. It might take a bit of time to find the job that does you justice, but in the meantime you need to be keeping that intellect of yours active and, like everybody else, you need money to be coming in. Am I right or am I right?"

"Yes, you are right, I guess," I say, knowing that this woman sounds exactly like my nan, "but I didn't do my degree and work hard in London just to do any old job, did I?"

I think that she must have been expecting this reaction, for she does not blink an eyelid. "Yes, but Nicholas," she says, smiling. She has a nice smile. "This is just a chance to get your feet back on the ground. And I don't really believe for one moment that you have really returned to Bridgend because, as it says here, you 'wanted the opportunity to contribute to the development of local employers.' You either messed up at your last job or you got messed up by some girl over there, yes?"

Damn, I'm thinking, does this girl need to be quite so honest and quite so right all the time?

"Okay," I say, holding up my hands, "maybe there are a few other reasons why I came home, which are not exactly detailed on the CV."

She looks pleased at my admission, a bit like a torturer who has just secured a confession from a hostage. Okay, well maybe not quite that pleased.

"Great," she says, crossing her legs. "So you're good then to start a job on Monday at national minimum wage, Nick?"

I hear myself saying yes.

Chapter Ten

Somebody's boring me. I think it's me – Dylan Thomas

"Yes, Mr Rogers, I completely appreciate your frustration," the girl says into her mouthpiece at the same time she examines her freshly painted pink nails. Never before has the female ability to multi-task been so evident. "And rest assured," she continues, indiscreetly checking her mobile phone for messages, "I will do my absolute utmost to provide a satisfactory resolution to your concerns as quickly as possible." The girl then turns to me, her eyes barely visible behind all the blue mascara, presses the mute button on the phone and says, "Some people just need to get a fucking life hey, pet?"

I've been working in my new role for two hours six minutes, and I calculate that I have five hours fifty-four minutes remaining before the end of my first shift, and whilst I'd be lying if I said it's been a roller-coaster ride of sensational highs and mind-blowing lows, I'm still in one piece and, to the best of my knowledge, I've not yet unintentionally told the boss to go fuck herself; which is something, I guess.

On arrival I sat in the foyer and observed the security guard giving a young lad, who looked like he was on work experience or something, a lecture on the importance of keeping his security card visible at all times. It was a bit of a David v Goliath battle, to be honest, only on this occasion I suspect that David would have gotten his sorry little ass kicked, sling or no sling. The boy looked like he'd been dressed by his mother, whilst the security guard, with his thick beard and gorilla-like frame, reminded me of a young Geoff Capes.

"Yes, I know that I see you every day, and I know that I know what your name is," he growled, "but that's not the point, is it?"

"Nick?"

A tall skinny guy probably in his early twenties stood over me. He had short curly hair that looked really tight and a big toothy smile. I stood up and shook his hand. The guy had big hands.

"My name is Mike. I'm the assistant team leader, for my sins."

Mike led me in the direction of the lifts. The lift doors closed just as we reached them. For some reason, Mike reminded me of the goalkeeper Petr Cech, and I had an image of him diving spectacularly to keep the doors open.

"Our boss, Pam, is in a meeting at the moment," Mike informed me as he pressed the button for the fourth floor, "and she wants to introduce you to the whole team personally a bit later. For now, if you just sit with Suzie and listen to some calls, it will hopefully give you a basic understanding of what we do. Pam can fill in the gaps for you later."

We walked into the office. I was in for a shock. It was open-plan, and looked massive. Absolutely everyone seemed to be busy talking into their headset. Sections were separated by wooden banners with team names. It flashed in big red letters on the wall how many calls were waiting and what the call waiting time was. I gulped. It was noisy. It was busy. There didn't seem to be anywhere you could chill out and hide for a while.

"This is Suzie," Mike said, directing my attention to a young blonde girl, a proper trophy wife. "Suzie, this is Nicholas. It is his first day as a temp today and we need you to look after him for a bit." Mike raised a single eye brow at me. The gesture was obvious. He was saying, *you lucky bastard.*

"No problems, Mike. Take a seat, sweetheart."

There was no doubt that Suzie was what would normally be considered a piece of skirt. Her long hair was bleached blonde to the point of being almost white. She had a golden tan which suggested that she'd just returned from a beach holiday, but more likely a tanning salon on the high street. Her eyes were an astonishing green. She undoubtedly had a slim, fit body hidden away behind the desk. You would certainly turn some eyes taking her out. I estimated that she was twenty-one, if that.

"It's a pleasure to meet you, Suzie," I said, a little too enthusiastically. I'd already decided that I was going to appear uniquely enthusiastic, mainly to camouflage the fact that, undoubtedly, I really didn't really give a damn. I went to shake Suzie's hand, but was only offered two limp fingers. She smiled meekly and then opened her drawer to pull out a bottle of hand wash. I wondered whether I should be offended. Suzie passed me a headset like it was a grenade about to explode.

"Just listen to a few calls, sweetheart, and you'll soon get the idea."

And true enough, I soon get the idea. Customers call with an enquiry. The advisor makes some sort of attempt, however token, to help. And then, once the customer is at least remotely satisfied (and there is quite a bit of flexibility with the 'remotely' aspect), the advisor tries to sell something the customer has no interest in buying.

"I appreciate that you are upset, Mr Jones, but unfortunately, I will not be able to continue the call if you persist in shouting at me." It was now that Suzie started applying the tinted nail polish. She was very delicate and precise with the brush.

"Fuck you!"

"Mr Jones, it is my responsibility to give you three warnings that your language is not acceptable. This is your second warning, Mr Jones."

"Fuck you!"

"Mr Jones, I regret to inform you that this is now your final warning. If you continue to use inappropriate language, I will unfortunately have no option but to terminate the call."

"Fuck you! Fuck you! Fuck you!"

Suzie terminated the call. It was two calls later I realised that it was only six minutes past eleven.

"So what do you do after work, Suzie?" I ask, trying to show an interest. Suzie looks at me with knowing eyes. She thinks I'm making some kind of move on her. She either imagines that I'm a Casanova, wasting no time in getting in there or, more likely, a bit desperate, like all the other guys in the office. I notice a streak of white just underneath her hairline. She's wearing fake tan.

"Gym, sweetheart. I go every night, don't I? Got to look after yourself, haven't you?"

That reminded me, Den told me that it's a good idea to eat a few nuts at regular intervals throughout the day because they keep your energy levels up. Which is ironic, really, because Den always looks half asleep. I open a miniature bag of almonds, eat one, and put the bag down on the desk.

A round lady in her fifties with square spectacles walks past laughing to herself.

"Oh, he has only been here five minutes and he has already got his nuts out on the table," she says, and starts cracking up.

Suzie raises her eye brows. "Oh, that's Karen," she says. "She's been here for like donkey's years, always done the same thing. She is nice enough but a bit mad, really. You'll soon get used to her."

A guy with a dimple in his chin and broad shoulders more commonly found on the wing for Wales drops a sheet of paper on the desk. It's some sort of performance update.

"Oh, hello, Gareth," Suzie says, brushing back her peroxide hair and jutting out her substantial cleavage. "How are you today?"

"Fine," the guy says, quickly moving onto the next desk.

"That's Gareth," Suzie explains. "He's such a nice guy."

Suzie goes to the rest area to get us a couple of drinks. She tells me that when she comes back, I can take a couple of calls; that Pam likes to get the temporary staff up and running as quickly as possible, that the best way to learn is to jump straight in at the deep end, and besides, she will be there to help me. I'm thinking that I really haven't got clue what I'm doing yet and I really am not ready to speak to anybody on the phone at all, but I don't want to appear cowardly or backward and so I just slur the words *sure, no problemo.*

A couple of guys on the next table follow her - or more accurately, follow her ass – with their eyes. The guys look like they are about nineteen. This place is starting to make me feel old. One of them gives me the thumbs up and then, kind of discreetly – well actually, no, not discreetly at all – mouths that I'm a lucky bastard.

Suzie returns and I take the headset. She is listening in. There is a buzzer in my ear. It may as well be a bell, signalling the first round of a boxing match against a double-hard bastard. I remind myself that I'm an exceptional individual devoted to change and development. No, hold on, Cath at the recruitment agency said that was bollocks, that it made me sound like a dick, didn't she? I press the call answer button on the phone.

"Welcome to *Gator Insurance*. My name is Nick Evans, your personal Customer Services Representative today, how can I help you, please?"

"Account number eight-seven-three-six-six-two-two-eight," a guy with a Manchester accent blurts at me.

I type in the digits but then realise that the numbers lock is not on.

"I am sorry, Sir," I say in my best posh voice. "There appears to have been a temporary systems error. Could you please repeat that number?"

"Which part?"

"All of it."

There is a pause of at least a couple of seconds when I'm sure he is shaking his head, before he repeats the number.

I type in the number again but it is still not recognised. "I am sorry, Sir, but the number is not recognised. Could you please repeat it for clarification?"

There is a deep sigh. The guy repeats the number again. The account details are still not recognised. I am beginning to feel flustered now.

"I'm sorry, Sir," I say, "but I cannot get it up."

"You cannot get it up?" the man repeats. His voice sounds different, somehow. "How long have you been having this problem?"

"I assure you it is not normally a problem. I just cannot get it up for you."

"For me?" he asks. "How do you think that makes me feel?"

I can hear the guy shouting to somebody, all jocular and jovial. *I've got a guy on the phone who says he can't get it up.* There's a laugh. *Tell him he can borrow some of my Viagra if he wants,* a voice shouts back.

Suzie leans forward and puts him on hold. Her perfume is overpowering. I know that my face is red and flushed. I'm definitely not feeling like an exceptional individual right now. London feels like a lifetime ago, a different lifetime in fact. It was a decent job, account managing these high-profile companies, I tell myself. I had a swagger about my step. I could talk the talk *and* walk the walk. Now I was being mocked by some random guy on the phone in a call centre for not being able to get it up. I think back to the kid with the security guard in the reception. If I was Goliath, even in my own small unimportant world, then I had definitely been felled, and now I felt like David, only without a sling.

A girl a couple of desks away smiles at me and gives me a wave. She has a friendly, pretty face and she is casually dressed and void of makeup. She seems full of bubbling energy. Life isn't so bad after all. I discreetly wave back. Now, though, the girl looks confused. She points at Suzie. She wasn't waving at me at all. Oh no, I think, actually, life just gets worse and worse. I wish that I could crawl under the desk and hide, only as I've already discovered in this place, with all of its modern open-plan ideas, there are no hiding places. I glance at the girl again and she is laughing now. She has her hand over her mouth to restrain her giggles, which appear to be overflowing.

She was only having a laugh. She was waving at me, after all. The relief is immense. And, I observe, this girl seems nice.

"You're doing just fine, sweetheart," Suzie says. "The guy probably has an old policy number. Just ask for his postcode and surname."

It is eleven forty-nine, and I have five hours and eleven minutes left until the end of my first shift.

London was easy compared to this. I already feel like a lie down.

Chapter Eleven

My parents have always been there for me, ever since I was about seven – David Beckham

It's just me and Den, in the sauna, down at the recreation centre.

I received the call-up first thing this morning. I had been lying in my boxers on the sofa, staring at a solitary cobweb in the corner of the room, playing a 'what if' game. 'What if' the first spider had created his or her very own family, with children and cousins and nieces and nephews? 'What if' the first spider had managed to cross the ocean in a wooden box from Brazil and was in fact a rare, poisonous species? 'What if' the family of spiders had been feeding on my protein shakes (to aid my developing bulk) and was now the size of a small to middling dog? I then remembered the old film from the eighties where the spiders turned out to be killers and the village fled screaming for their lives. When my phone (which was balancing precariously on my forehead) vibrated, I was relieved to be given an escape route from this house of horrors.

Den was sounding lively and enthusiastic, and so I wondered what was up. His usual Saturday morning five-a-side football set-up was a player short, he said, and he wondered whether I could be pulled into the fray. It didn't matter if I couldn't, he added; they would just need to cancel, and the nine other players would be just fine about it, no problems at all. I was his first choice, he said, as I'd always been a good player and all that. I wondered firstly what this 'all that' was about and, secondly, if I was such an obvious choice, then why had I only been asked to play when they were a player down? But then, I mused, I wasn't exactly what could traditionally be called 'busy', even if my intellectual capacity was working over time. And so, I agreed to play.

The other nine turned out to be quite a serious bunch. They wore tight vests and stretched their groins and shouted encouragement to each other before kick-off. One of the players, a tall skinny guy with a hairy neck, even wore a white sweatband round his head. It was, I thought, only supposed to be a Saturday morning kick-around amongst friends. A green, musty curtain divided the hall in two. The polished concrete slabs were covered in red and yellow stripes, outlining the badminton courts. At either end of the court were basketball nets. It wasn't exactly the cup final at Wembley between Cardiff City and Portsmouth. Apparently, though, the two teams had been battling it out every week, without fail, for just under a year, and they were on an even keel.

Standing on the pitch in my tight black shorts, my legs looking whiter and my knees wobblier than I could ever remember, I realised that I hadn't kicked a football, let alone a yellow furry one, in what must be years. But as soon as the whistle blew, there wasn't time to worry; there wasn't time to think. I started doing basic things pretty well, like passing the ball to somebody standing right next to me, and then gradually more difficult things, like shooting at goal. It quickly became apparent that I was holding my own. When I scored a goal, I received a high-five from one of the serious players. It was going well.

And the game was close. The goals were going in at a rapid rate at both ends but, amazingly, there was only ever one goal between the two teams. The hairs on my legs glistened with sweat, and adrenaline pumped through my body. There were a couple of kids behind the goal, just strays with presumably nothing better to do on a Saturday afternoon, no doubt, and they started commentating on the game, like they were John Motson. Every player was given the name of a contemporary player from the top leagues in Europe; in the world. *That's a great pass by Messi to Rooney*, they exclaimed, and *oh I say what a crunching tackle by Didier Drogba* (Den, naturally); all that sort of crazy stuff. And yet they struggled for ages to give me a name, to match me with a suitable player from the top flight of football. Eventually, just after I'd taken a speculative shot at goal, I was downbeat to hear one of the little shits shout *and Peter Crouch shoots harmlessly wide.*

Peter fucking Crouch!

Regardless, there were only seconds left, and the game was tied at eleven each. The large digital clock high up on the wall ticked down from ten, nine, eight seconds. I put in a crunching tackle on the half way line and regained possession. *Oh I say, Evans effortlessly glides the ball past another player.* A quick 'Matthew's shuffle' and the goal opened up in front of me. The clock clicked down five, four seconds. This was my moment of glory. This was my own, personal cup final.

Only, for the first time in the whole game, there was time to think, even as the clock ticked down to three, two seconds. The goal seemed smaller than before, the goalkeeper much bigger, my legs much, much heavier. I couldn't see any empty net to kick the ball at. And so I just kicked the ball as hard as I could.

I don't believe it; Peter Crouch has bottled it. He's put the ball over the bar, and in the dying seconds of the game, as well!

And now, forty-five minutes later (a full half of a game) the other eight players have gone their separate ways and it is just me and Den in the sauna, in silence. The two teams are still on an even keel, ready to battle out another game one week from today.

I know it sounds like an obvious thing to say, but it's steaming hot in this sauna. Den has the coldest blood of any man that I have ever known, and he has been pouring the water into the coals like it was going out of fashion. I watch him lean forward, his impossibly tight bathers stretching and straining (and I'm hoping and praying that one of his balls doesn't pop out), as he picks up the little shovel yet again and adds even more water. The fog becomes so thick that my friend becomes just a faint outline, somewhere over there.

"You were wicked today, big man; all the lads were well impressed," he says.

I feel my pigeon chest pump out with pride. I *was* good, I

tell myself, despite the sitter at the end. It feels like a while since I was paid a compliment.

"Cheers mate. It's just a pity about the miss at the end, hey."

"You made the miss yourself, Nick," he says, and I think this is a compliment. "I was hiding at the back, hoping that the ball did not come to me, praying that I wasn't given an opportunity that could cost us a win. But you put yourself right out there. You were the braver man, man."

I hadn't thought of it like that. It was only a Saturday morning kick around, after all, and yet I knew that to some of the guys, and Den included, it meant a whole lot more.

I wonder about Den now, though. Right now he just seems to talk a good game, like a commentator who knows all about every type of zonal marking, but who has never actually kicked a ball in his life. There is plenty of commendable analysis and rationality, but none of it progresses towards a career he enjoys or a woman he loves and can call his own, does it? What does this guy have to be proud of? But there again, I tell myself, what is important to me might not be important to him. It's really none of my business, yeah? But it's at this point that I really get stuck, because however hard I try to justify his current life, which, let's be honest, is a million miles away from all the things I used to have, I just cannot convince myself that my friend actually *is* happy.

He even seems to be envious of me for missing a sitter in the last second of a five-a-side football match down the local recreation centre, for example. My life isn't going anywhere fast; after all; I'm living at home with my parents, I've no girlfriend and I'm working in a call centre for peanuts. And to think of all the things I had in London. I really was a bit of a catch then, for sure. But Den definitely seems to be looking up to me, living this life now. And it's always, always been the other way around.

He wasn't always this guy with no drive or aspiration. In school, he was always a bit of a swot, which seems crazy thinking about it now. Most of the kids would mess around in class, but I remember Den, always at the front, with his back straight, his head upright, listening intently. He seemed oblivious to the other kids flicking rubbers and elastic bands all around him. The problem was, putting it as politely, he wasn't really all that gifted academically. I had a problem remembering things, but with Den he didn't really understand a lot of it in the first place. The one subject he was always good at, surprisingly, was Welsh. The other kids would imitate him, behind his back, of course, speaking Welsh in his Jamaican drawl. To be honest, it was dead funny.

I never really understood, though, why he didn't take Welsh for A-Level. It was the one subject he'd aced at GCSE. He said something about his parents wanting him to do solid subjects, and he ended up doing Maths, chemistry and economics, which he'd only just about managed to scrape through at GCSE. I did economics with him, and I always remember him sitting next to me in the exam hall looking absolutely panic stricken, his eyes red and filled with dread. He failed all his A-Level exams and didn't go to university, and instead got a job in a bank in town instead. To the best of my knowledge he hasn't taken another exam since.

"So I would have thought that Patrick would have been playing, mate?"

They've always been close, Den and his older brother Patrick. He's really into the family stuff. I guess it's a cultural thing. His mum and dad came over from Jamaica in the early eighties – originally to London – and I think there is a strong sense of solidarity; that they are all in this together. And yet he hasn't mentioned Patrick much since I've been back in Bridgend.

"He did play a couple of times, but he didn't get on too well with some of the lads, man. He can go a bit crazy, you know, like? And he is into all the bodybuilding stuff nowadays. Nobody wants to deal with an angry guy who's just had a protein shake for breakfast. Not on your day off."

I'm a bit surprised by this, if only because Patrick is one of the most laid-back guys I'd ever met. He makes Den look like a nervy type who lives on a diet of cappuccino and *Red*

Bull. It is hard to imagine Patrick mustering enough energy to get angry and, as for the bodybuilding; he seems too lazy to pump weights, and he's always been powerfully built anyway. But then I'd always thought the same about Den, and right now his arms remind me of tree trunks, all thick and sturdy.

"What's with all the Jamaican and Welsh stuff then, geezer?"

I'm referring, on his occasion, to his earrings. His left ear has a stud with the red and white of Wales, and the right a stud with the green and yellow of Jamaica. At one point during the game, when one of our players tried to jump on his back after he had scored a goal, Den warned him "Don't be confused by the earring!"

"The countries will always be major for me, man. Jamaican blood runs through my veins. But I was born and bred in Wales. It's just my way of showing respect; get where I'm at?"

I nod my head, but I doubt he can see me through the mist.

"I tell you," Den continues, "plenty of Welsh ladies have enjoyed the full benefit of these Jamaican genes." He laughs wickedly, and it reminds me of his older brother at his best. "Funny thing, though," he says, "I picked up a girl the other night, and before I knew it, her tits were out, her fanny was wet, and I was going down on her. Anyway, before that, when she pulled down my kegs she looked a bit disappointed. Now I've never known a girl be disappointed by the junk inside my trunk; I'm Jamaican, after all! So I asked this girl what was up, and she said, all husky like but with a thick Welsh accent, 'oh, you've shaved your balls, haven't you? I prefer it all natural.' And right then, I knew that I was going to be dealing with one hairy fanny, man."

I'm chuckling like a little schoolgirl at this. "I'll get straight to the point. I won't beat around the bush," I say, impressed by my own hilarity. "Was it?"

"Never had so many pubic hairs in my mouth at one time," Den replies, matter-of-factly. "And remember," he continues. "I've dated girls from the valleys."

Den has hundreds of these stories. I've never dared ask how many women he has slept with, just because I know that it is a hell of a lot more than me. It is something that he prides himself on. I guess it's the more women you pull the bigger man you are, type of thing.

I change the subject again.

"You heard those kids on the side of the pitch. So which footballer would you most like to be like, Den?"

"David Beckham," he says, without any hesitation.

"Why's that?" I ask. It could be the way he is Captain Marvel, I think, leading England by example, or maybe even the way he curls his free kicks?

"All the chicks love Becks, Nick," Den says. "Hell," he continues, leaning forward to grab the water shovel, and once again I'm amazed by how he managed to fit inside those tiny bathers, "I'm as straight as the next man, but even I'd shag David Beckham! More heat, Nick?"

No, I think; this is definitely time to go have a shower.

Chapter Twelve

Grown ups are complicated creatures, full of quirks and secrets – Roald Dahl

I'm always surprised just how depressing hospitals can be. I know my expectations should be pretty low because, well, they are obviously full of sick people.

The heels of my leather shoes tap against the tiled floor. There must be ketchup on my chin or toothpaste coating my mouth, because everyone walking the opposite direction seems to be staring straight at me. The walls of the endless corridor are covered with paintings from the local primary school. The theme is the family. I glance at one of the paintings and conclude that the five-year-old girl is not yet an accomplished painter. Either that or her dad is Andre the Giant, her mother a little pixie and their family pet is a lion. Knowing the area, I'd put my money on the Andre the Giant option.

Den told me once that he always associates hospitals with the smell of disinfectant and boiled cabbage. I joked that the disinfectant is probably needed after the patients have eaten the boiled cabbage, but he didn't laugh. Tonight, however, the smell of disinfectant and cabbage has been overpowered by the distinctive scent of gloss paint. The skirting boards have been painted a bright, shiny white. Maybe they are trying to cheer the place up. It sure as fuck doesn't work.

I'm looking for Ward East 17. I consider asking whether pop music is allowed in the ward, but it doesn't feel appropriate and, more appropriately, there isn't anyone to actually ask. I'm here on my own. My father's words replay in my mind. *You may be a bit shocked when you see her, son.* I'd managed to blank everything out and just continue in automatic-pilot mode. With every tap of my leather shoe, with every step closer to East 17, however, the more real it is becoming, and the more scared I feel.

I rub the sterilising lotion into my hands and then poke my head inside the room. There are about eight beds on both sides. Blank, confused faces stare back at me. My eyes dart from one bed to the next. That isn't her. That isn't her. Not that one, either. No, hold on. That one *is* her.

I walk over to my nan. She is sat upright on a bed, back propped up against a pillow. The sheets are white and her dressing gown is a sickly green. She notices me and her face breaks into a smile. My nan waves at me. I wonder what my dad was going on about. She doesn't seem so bad.

"Hello Nan," I say, planting a wet kiss on her cheek. "It's Nick, your favourite grandson."

Nan looks at me ruefully. "You are my only grandson," she says.

The woman on the bed next to her looks up from a crossword and chuckles. She is about ninety and there's some dribble on her chin. I hope she doesn't come out with a 'if I was fifty years younger' line.

"Exactly," I say. "There is no disputing that I am your favourite."

I take a moment to adjust to my new surroundings. I move the black plastic seat closer to the bed and hold her hand. It feels bony and the skin is painfully thin. There is a half drunk glass of orange juice, a couple of newspapers and about twelve or so cards on the table next to the bed. The wedding photo is there, too, which is nice. I gaze at Nan in the prime of her life, looking like a movie star, and at the little girl at the front, in a fancy dress, beaming the most fantastic smile. The little girl is my Aunt Sally, a chain smoking woman nowadays with more lines across her face than a zebra. I hope that I never get old, I think. I consider reaching for the paper and browsing through it, just like I would if I visited Nan at home, but think better of it. I notice that the crossword on the back page has already been completed. There is a placard with her full name on the bed railing.

"Famous at last then, Nan," I say.

She is still smiling.

"Infamous more like."

"So, how are you feeling, then?" I ask. It feels like the

most appropriate question, seeing as she is in hospital and all.

"Better than I have in years," she says. "I've no idea why these quacks are keeping me here. I've got loads of things I could be getting on with."

"What have you got to be getting on with?" I ask, sincerely.

She squeezes my hand; thinks for a moment. "That's not the point," she says. "I'd prefer to be doing nothing in my own home, thank you very much, than doing nothing in a place that smells of cabbage and disinfectant."

I notice than she is speaking faster than usual. She also seems, well, happier. It must be the drugs, I think. Maybe they have put her on morphine or something. The 'something' is quite general, because really, I haven't a clue what drugs they would put her on.

"Did you know that morphine is named after the Greek god Morpheus, Nan?" I ask.

Nan is usually interested in little snippets of information. She makes mental notes, ready to use in a crossword later. Admittedly, this one is a bit random, but it's what came to mind. She looks at me now like I've lost the plot. In fact, her eyes wander over my face in complete fascination, like she is wondering who this crazy guy at the end of her bed is.

"What the *fuck* does that have to do with anything, Nick?" she asks.

I've heard my nan swear before. Never like this though. I'm a bit shocked.

Then she puts her head back and starts laughing. Her nose wrinkles and her cheeks crease. The woman on the next bed puts down her crossword again and starts chuckling, too. I don't think she even heard what was said; I think she just likes chuckling. I start laughing, too.

"You always were a silly little sausage, Nick," my nan says, affectionately.

A nurse comes over to the bed. There is a small brown stain on her light blue uniform, just below the chest. I wonder what it is. She is pretty enough, though, with thick brown hair scraped back, and a sprinkling of freckles on her forehead. Probably about my age, I think. As she passes the bed, I notice that her ass is disproportionately large compared to the rest of her body, which is usually a bonus, even though generally I prefer my girls tall and slim.

"I hope that this one has been behaving herself?" she says to me.

"Piss off," my nan bleats. There is a deathly pause, before she starts laughing hysterically again.

"I'm sorry about that," I say, more than a tad embarrassed.

"Don't worry, she is a real character, this one, aren't you, Joyce?" she says, fussing about the bed.

"And Toni is such a very nice girl," my nan says. "She has been ever so nice to me." Nan smiles mischievously and nods her head in the direction of Toni. It crosses my mind that maybe she is trying to set me up.

"She seems a little high," I comment to Toni.

She smiles at me. It is a nice, warm smile. "That is perfectly normal. She is on drugs because of the stroke."

"It was definitely a stroke, then?" I ask.

Toni looks at me a little concerned now. "Oh, yes, it was definitely a stroke."

I absorb the information and absent-mindedly follow the trail of her ass out of the room.

"Yes, Nick, it definitely is a big one," my nan says, as if reading my mind.

The woman next door starts laughing again.

"How's your mum?" my nan asks. "We don't talk any more, you know."

For the first time, I notice that there is a definite slur in her voice. She never discusses not talking to my mum. Never. I wonder whether it's the stroke or the drugs talking right now.

Of course, I've always wondered why they don't talk. As a kid I became determined to find out why, and I conjured up all sorts of weird and wonderful storylines, most of them taken straight from *Eastenders*. It was mission impossible, though, as I didn't have the guts to ask either of them. And so I gave up. I just accepted it as one of the unchangeable facts of life. The world is round. The sea is blue. Mum and Nan don't talk. I figured that if I was supposed to know, one of them would have told me.

But now Nan is talking. All she knows is the truth.

"So why don't you, you know....?" I begin to ask, but I instantly regret it. She is vulnerable. She is high on drugs. This is just wrong. I respect her too much.

"Why don't we what dear? Why don't we talk?"

"No, not that, Nan, not that..." I flail, desperately backtracking.

There is a flicker in my nan's eyes. My whole body tenses. This is it. This is the moment I find out. I don't want to know. Not anymore. It was all okay when I just didn't know.

"You'll have to ask your mum," my Nan says, matter-of-factly, and the relief is immense, it is awesome.

"She is very concerned about you," I say, trying to move the talk forward, not giving her enough time to change her mind. This part is true. I've heard my mum and dad whispering. My mum is not the sort of person to whisper. She's been staring into space in the garden, too. My mum is usually moving, always on the go.

"Yes, she always was a worrier," my nan says. Her face rotates in a full circle, like it is not controlled by the neck. Her lip quivers. She wants to say something else, I can tell.

"Your father was here earlier," she says. "He is such a good man, that one. You really should look up to him more, you know."

She is right; I know that, I just find it difficult. I know that he is a nice, genuine man. It's just to me he has always been my safe, dull dad.

My nan looks a bit anxious now. She shuffles around under the sheets, her feet kicking out. For a brief moment the bedcover falls below her waist. She quickly and desperately swipes at it with her left hand. She is not quick enough, though. I have time to notice that something is not quite right with the other arm. It's as though it is just hanging there, lifeless.

I try to act normal, as if nothing had happened.

"I do love you, Nan," I say.

She looks at me now, her face completely still. There are no tics. Her eyes are watering.

"I know, Nick," she says. "And I love you, too."

The corridor seems even longer on the way back. My mum opens the front door of the house before I have even managed to put the key in the lock. She has been waiting. Her normally immaculate appearance looks a bit uncoordinated. Her hair is out of place, her lipstick has not been drawn in a perfect straight line.

She makes me a cup of tea as if nothing has changed and then sits down opposite.

"How is she?" she asks.

"She is absolutely fine, Mum," I lie.

Chapter Thirteen

In terms of the 'S' word, that does not enter my mind. And it never has done. In terms of An Attempt. Because I am stronger than that. I might be a weak person, but I can take pain – Richey Edwards, missing member of Manic Street Preachers

I stopped dead; considered turning around and running in the opposite direction, and then hiding - hiding somewhere I could never, ever be found. But no; instead I froze. One foot moved back but the other moved forward, so that I ended up doing a fancy jiggle on the spot and not moving anywhere at all. It was like the gym hall on a cold wet Thursday afternoon all over again. The woman saw me. The eyes were initially glazed, but then they lit and flickered with recognition. *Count to ten, ready or not, I'm coming to find you.* There was no turning back now. The hiding was over. I had been found.

I had joined the leisure centre about four weeks ago. My work trousers were getting smaller. I'd always been used to being skinny, and so initially the extra pounds were sort of welcome. Then it dawned on me that having skinny arms and legs and a little pot belly was probably not a good look. The belt was now merely a fashion accessory; the trousers were staying up just fine on their own, thank you very much. Now I needed an inhale of breathe just to get them on. I asked my mum, quite reasonably, I felt, whether the clothes were shrinking in the wash. She replied that either the clothes were getting smaller or I was getting bigger. And then she added, a tad unnecessarily, that *her* clothes fitted just fine.

And so, the very next day, I joined the gym.

I've been going pretty regularly, too, which was probably the biggest surprise; usually once or twice in the week but, like today, always on Sunday mornings, and then back in time for my Mum's Sunday roast. My belt was back in action and actually serving a real purpose, and even my arms are getting thicker. I'd just finished my workout and showered and changed and was briskly heading towards the exit, when I saw her.

"Hello, Nick," Mrs Thornton, or as I have always known her - Sam's mum – said to me, smiling breezily. "It's been a long time. You're all grown up," she laughed.

I struggled to keep eye contact. In fact, I struggled to keep still at all. My hands fidgeted and twisted and I bounced on the balls of my feet.

"Hello, Mrs Thornton," I'd said, smiling and trying to look as calm and sane as possible. "How are you?"

"Very well, thank you Nick, all things considering," she said, still maintaining her smile.

There was a pause. It was probably only a couple of seconds, but it felt like a couple of lifetimes. I shifted uneasily, putting my weight on one side and then on the other. I thought about just saying how nice it was to see her again and walking – jogging – running - off.

"Nick, would you mind having a coffee or something with me? You'd be doing me a great favour, if truth be told."

And what exactly was there to say to that? I had not seen his kind, lovely woman since before Sam had gone went missing. And Sam – her *only* son – was still missing, for God's sake. There was no way that I could say no, although, to be fair, I did think about it. Actually, that's not quite right. I *could* have said no. I could have made an excuse, said that I had a lunch date or an urgent meeting or something. But that absolutely, undoubtedly, would have been the wrong thing to say.

"Of course," I said. "That would be nice."

And so here we are, overlooking the swimming pool with all of the excited, splashing, screaming kids, sipping hot chocolate and coffee, a strong smell of chlorine in the air.

I'd thought about Mrs Thornton so many times since Sam vanished. In my imagination, she'd become a drunk, a wreck; a mad woman. Her days were spent alone in darkened rooms, rocking back and forth in a tatty chair, and her nights were spent aimlessly wandering the streets, hopelessly looking for answers. But, looking at this attractive, sane woman sat in front of me now, the fantasy definitely does not seem to match the reality. Mrs Thornton looks fit and healthy, both physically and mentally.

Mrs Thornton was the mum we all fancied. Of course, we all pretended to fancy everyone's mum, even though some of them seemed to be related to *Shrek* in some way. We'd been brought up on mother jokes, in the same way that other children might be brought up on Catholicism or Manchester United. The only difference with Mrs Thornton was that, deep down, we weren't joking at all. We all actually *did* want to shag her.

In my early daydreams, the perfect mate's mother would be someone like Nigella Lawson; a super-mum who always looks sensational and yet never ever breaks into a sweat, a mum who jumps out of bed as soon as that alarm goes off at six without bleary eyes and the remains of last night's makeup, eager to make a fulfilling breakfast and pack a nutritious lunchbox combining both fruit and wholemeal, who bakes biscuits in the evening and helps with the maths homework. The sort of mum that all other mums, without exception, absolutely hate. *How does she do it all and still look so good,* they gossip outside the school gates. *Mind you, I think she has put a bit of weight on her hips,* they bitch.

And yet Mrs Thornton was nothing like that. She couldn't cook, for a start. I'm also sure she wouldn't have been able to help Sam with his maths homework. Sam was the best student in the whole year at maths. Whereas Den and I struggled with our work, Sam really was a natural. And as a single working mother, she had to struggle, and she never pretended any different. For sure, though, she was younger, cooler and sexier than all the other mums. And not only that, she was such a sweet lady, too. I'm sure that the other mums never bitched about her outside the school gates.

I remembered the first time I went to Sam's house for tea, and she opened the door. She may as well have had a halo above her head. My jaw dropped and my ears burned. She was only petite, maybe 5'3 if she was wearing say, two inch heels or something; a tiny slip of a woman. But she had this big smile that spread from cheek to cheek and these pale blue eyes that sparkled. And it was pretty obvious to any thirteen year old boy that, hiding underneath those baggy joggers was one hot body.

"Mate, your mum is a MILF!" I exclaimed to Sam as soon as we were out of earshot.

"Whatever," he said, but you could tell he knew I was right. How hard must that be, conceding that your own mum is hot?

"Where's your dad?"

"No dad," he replied, simply.

"Mind if I have a crack, then?" I asked, daringly.

With most other boys, this would have earned me a punch on the arm or at least a nipple twist, but then, Sam wasn't like most other boys. He just smiled at me pitifully, just like a twenty-year-old girl probably does when an old man gives her the eye.

"I'm pretty sure my mum will be able to resist your thirteen-year-old charms, especially as most thirteen-year-old girls seem to be able to, Nick," he said, annoyingly old beyond his years.

"Maybe just a blow job, then, yeah?" I retorted, trying to push my luck. And this time, to be fair, Sam *did* twist my nipples (both of them, if I remember) and I quickly shut up.

"So what are you here for today then Mrs Thornton?" I ask now, thirteen years (another lifetime for that thirteen-year-old boy) or so later.

"Please, call me Jan," she (Mrs Thornton) instructs me, pouting her red lips. "I'm just here for a LBT class; I go every Sunday. I go to classes most night of the week nowadays."

Despite myself and the situation, I'd already checked out her legs, bum and tum when I followed behind her to the café, and now it was fair to say that the class must be working.

"I prefer a BLT," I nervously joke. "Bacon, lettuce and tomato!"

Mrs Thornton smiles, and it seems genuine enough.

"Well, I must say, you are looking very well," I

awkwardly offer. And just like they did all those years earlier, my ears burn red.

"That's very nice of you to say, Nick," Mrs Thornton says, and she does seem flattered. Her middle finger circles the outline of her cup. "You are not looking too bad yourself, you know. I remember when you first came to the house with Sam. You must have been about twelve or thirteen. You were just a skinny little thing then," she laughs.

It's the first time that either of us has mentioned Sam, even though we both know he is the only reason we are here and talking now.

"I remember that," I say. "You cooked us chips with fish fingers and beans."

"Oh, listen to you," Mrs Thornton says, presumably impressed by my memory for all things culinary. "That makes sense, though," she continues. "That's what I cooked most nights of the week."

When Sam came to our house for the first time, my mum laid the table in the dining room (we usually ate in the kitchen) and she cooked an extravagant steak meal (we usually ate something from the freezer). It was absolutely imperative that she made a good impression; that Sam went home and told his mother how welcome she had made him feel. But Mrs Thornton wasn't like that at all. She was just herself. I'm sure that dinner that night was just like it was every other night of the week

"I remember when you came over for Halloween and Sam crayoned your face blue."

I remember that too. We were thirteen, and to be honest, veterans on the trick or treating scene. We only went to try and get some extra cash and get into some egg fights with some younger kids. I was going as an ugly witch, with green face and warts and yellow teeth (to be honest, just like a lady I pulled in town a few years later). Sam crayoned my face in the low light in the hall, and when he turned the light on, we discovered that he had coloured my face blue and not green. We thought, *to hell with it,* let's go anyway. But the first door we knocked on some big geezer in a muscle vest opened the door and said *who have you come as*

– a Mr Man? And aren't you twenty-one or something? We gave up after that.

She asks me what I do now, and I tell her about London, about Katie, about my temporary ongoing job that just seems to be ongoing and ongoing, and she laughs and nods her head and coos and ahs in all the right places. I don't feel the need to elaborate or stretch the truth too much.

A little boy in pink (yes, pink) Speedos takes a run and jumps into the pool, splashing water over us. Mrs Thornton laughs and wipes the water from her cheeks. Then her eyes dart quickly from side to side and she leans forward.

"Do you think about him much?" she asks, almost whispering.

I pause before answering. "Yes, I do," I say.

"They think he committed suicide, you know," she says. For once, her blue eyes are not looking at me. They stare intently at the coffee cup, at the swimming pool, at anything *but* me.

I think of something to say. I take a deep breath, ready to speak, but then it dawns on me that there is absolutely nothing that I *can* say. I just nod my head and then, for the first time, I do something without thinking. I reach forward and take hold of her hand. It's not to make the right impression. It's what I want to do.

She looks straight in my eyes now. Her own eyes are bloodshot. There is a smear of black mascara as a tear trickles down her cheek. "They are wrong, you know," she says simply. "I know that Sam is still alive."

"How do you – I'm sorry – I mean…"

She looks at me kindly, squeezes my hand tighter. "It's okay," she says. "A mother knows when her son is still alive."

I know that this is the real Mrs Thornton talking. She *has* changed, after all. The woman I met when I was thirteen did not care what others thought of her. There was no need to make a good impression. She was just a single mother trying to do the best she could. Now, all the exercise classes and the pride in her appearance is her way of saying to the rest of the world that she is okay, that she is coping just fine. It is to mask what must be – just *has* to be – more inner torment than I could ever even fathom. And I guess she *is* coping, in her own way.

I want to believe her, really I do, but it has been so long and all the evidence indicates that he is dead, that I just can't.

We are outside, and it is grey. Mrs Thornton shakes my hand and then, after a pause, she hugs me. Her grip is surprisingly firm for such a small woman.

"I feel so much better after talking to you, Nick," she says. Her eyes are no longer bloodshot. She looks pretty again, just like I always remember her.

"I do, too," I say.

And I give her my number and tell her that if she ever wants to talk, I will be there. And I know that I will be, too.

Watching her walking to her car, I'm glad that I didn't hide; that, count to ten, ready or not, she found me.

Chapter Fourteen

I learnt to say 'hello handsome' in Dutch. I was making all the boys say it, not telling them what it meant – Cerys Matthews

I'm waiting for my dad to pick me up from work, standing on the side of the road, watching the cars whizz by.

There were a few highlights in the day. My two o'clock meeting with my new Manager, Pam, for starters. I'd only just finished my lunch (a Chinese chicken baguette) and I was more concerned with my breath than anything that might be discussed in the meeting.

Pam Harris is notorious in the office. In her own small world, she is famous. Everybody knows her, from the security guards who open the doors in the morning, to the cleaners at night who turn the lights off.

Her exact age is uncertain. She has either had a hard life (born an orphan, worked in the steel mill from the age of six, for example) and she is an old fifty-five, or she has had a wonderful life and is more like, say, seventy-three or something. Pam is not what you would ordinarily call a good looking woman – her nose is probably half an inch too long, and her eyes are set possibly half an inch too wide, but she is most definitely what you'd call a *respectable* looking woman. My mother would say that there goes a lady who takes pride in her appearance. Her salt and pepper hair is always perfectly in place, and her mascara and lipstick is always immaculately applied.

What makes her well known in the office is her absolute and unquestioned commitment to the company. She lives, breathes and sleeps *Gator Insurance*. Some of the other managers work hard, but none of them are in the same league as Pam Harris. She is first to arrive in the office (after the security) and last in the office to leave (sometimes even after the cleaners). There was a rumour that she spent most of her holiday in Crete last summer texting ideas to the Performance Manager. On the one hand, her commitment is respected by the few, but on the other, it is mocked by the many. The common consensus is that all her hard work would be better committed elsewhere. None of the youngsters, for example, have great aspirations to be doing the job at her age. As Suzie so eloquently said on my first day, *some people just need to get a fucking life, hey pet?*

"So, how do you think you are getting on, Nick?" Pam asked, leaning forward, twisting her fingers together.

"I'm really enjoying it," I replied.

It was a closed question, really. What else could I say? Thinking about it, I do remember this one lad at University who might have given a different answer. He used to wander around campus on his own a fair bit. We felt a bit of a connection, I guess, because I wandered around on my own a fair bit, too. We became nodding acquaintances, but no more. One time I saw him and, thinking I'd make a bit of an effort, said "you alright, mate?" thinking he would say "alright, mate" back, or maybe "fine thanks, mate, and you?" Only, this guy stopped and started chatting. He told me that, actually, he wasn't alright, he was far from alright; things really weren't going all that well at all, blah-de-blah. I thought, no wonder you're wandering around on your own all the time. Anyway, my point is, if there is a point at all, I can't think of anyone else I've met who would have given a different answer.

"That's good to hear, Nick," Pam said, with a genuine enough smile. "How are you getting on with the rest of the team? I hope that you feel we are a welcoming crowd, even if we can be a little wild and crazy at times."

She made it sound like half the team were sniffing glue in the toilet in between taking calls. It never crossed my mind that the team was anything close to being wild and crazy.

There is her assistant, Mike (aka. Petr Cech). He's a nice guy, and very keen, but his age and goofiness goes against him. None of the guys take him seriously and they always take the piss. Mike is officially Pam's assistant, but he's on the same grade as the rest of the team. Everyone refers to him as Teacher's Pet or, worse I guess, Golden Balls.

Suzie is the attraction for the young guys. She's alright, in all honesty. She is always friendly and helpful and I think she has a soft touch for me. She does her job and goes home. It is pretty obvious that she doesn't have any real interest in the place, though.

Karen stands out like a sore thumb, but she makes me laugh and I like her. She is crude to the point of being crass. For example, on my second week, she asked me whether I'd watched the Wales match on the weekend. She seemed to have a good knowledge of the game and was talking tactics and the like. It was all going swimmingly. Then, without warning, she said something along the lines of, "that Australian referee, what's his name? Steve something-or-other, I think it is. I tell you, Nick, he is sex in a bun, that one. Good God, give me a bun and I'll stick him in it, oh yes…"

And then, last but definitely not least, there's the girl who waved to me when I was taking that difficult call on my first day.

"The team has really helped me settle in," I said. "And don't worry, Pam," I continued with a wry smile, "I can be a little wild and crazy, too."

"I'm sure you can, Nick," Pam replied unconvincingly. "And how do you feel your performance has been coming along?"

"I think it's been improving. There aren't too many things that cause me problems any more. And I'm trying to utilise the support and knowledge that is available from the rest of the staff."

"Well, I've listened to some of your calls, and you certainly have a wonderful telephone manner. You build an instant rapport with the caller. Your tone is considerate and polite, which, of course, is all very encouraging."

I nod my head and smile, which, again, is the only appropriate thing to do.

"But…"

As soon as you hear that three letter-word, you know that

things are going to go downhill. On this occasion, the slope was steeper than the wooden roller coaster at Oakwood.

"But, Nick," Pam began, "we are now officially a National Sales Centre, which means that every member of staff has a responsibility both to themselves and the company to sell to the customers. Naturally, our expectations for you are lower because you are new to the company and so you will be improving all the time. However, taking that into account, your sales figure are still disappointing, Nick."

Oh. I wasn't actually expecting this.

I asked how much I actually had sold.

"You haven't sold anything at all, Nick."

Oh. This was actually a bit of a shocker. The reality, when I thought about it, was that I had never actually gotten around to selling anything. It had taken me a bit of time to get used to the systems and the questions the customers asked. Once I had sort of figured that out, I guess I *forgot* that I was supposed to be selling. I felt a little embarrassed now, especially because, as Pam said, it was fairly obvious I was supposed to be selling, seeing that I was working in a Sales Centre.

But once I had gotten over the initial shock-horror, I wasn't too concerned. I gave my assurances to Pam, and she seemed satisfied enough. Now that I'd remembered that I was actually supposed to be selling, I knew that I could do it well enough. After all, my ability for relentless charm and deceit had been tutored by that charming, deceitful bastard Paul, in London.

And it wasn't all bad. There was still that girl who had waved at me when I was taking that difficult call on my very first day.

Her name, as it turns out, is Sara.

I was in the drinks room after my meeting, drowning my sorrows with a very milky hot chocolate, standing with a hand on my hip, looking a bit lost, no doubt.

"Hello, handsome," she said, as she glided into the room. Her lips looked red and full and her smile was just so irresistibly cute. Standing up, she is hardly any taller than when she sits down. The girl must be less than five feet tall, but this merely gives her a fascinating pixie look, especially with her spiky brown hair and ears that point out a little more than normal.

"Oh, hello, Sara," I said back, probably blushing.

Sara looked at me confused. Her eyes narrowed and that irresistibly cute smile vanished into nothing.

"I wasn't saying hi to you!" she said. "I was talking to Bill."

I glanced over my shoulder and Bill, a guy with a grizzly beard and an even grizzlier demeanour, was struggling with the chocolate machine (shaking it with both his hands, in fact).

"Oh, I'm sorry," I said, looking to the floor for support.

But when I dared look up again, that smile had returned. Only, this time it was even more irresistible than a moment ago.

"I'm *fucking* with you, handsome. See you later, Nick," she said, swivelling her hips and almost skipping back to her desk.

A car pulls up on the side of the road. There is a beep of the horn.

We veer out of Cardiff and onto the A48. When my dad is in the car with my mum, he is notorious for being a slow driver. My mum scares the life out of him, warning him of pedestrians walking on the pavement that could walk out into the road at any time or bikes that could make unexpected manoeuvres. We got overtaken by a tractor once. It is no wonder that the poor man spends all his time pottering around in the shed. Now that she is not here, though, he is actually quite nifty. It is quite funny the effect my mum has on him.

It was at breakfast this morning that Dad suggested he pick me up from work. "I could pick you up from work," he said. I was eating my toast at the time. There wasn't any reason why he couldn't pick me up, I thought, but then, being a retired council worker or whatever, there wasn't any reason why he couldn't pick me up any other day, either.

"Ooh, that will be nice, won't it, Nick?" Mum instantly cooed

My mother had spoken. So here we are.

"Good day at work, Nick?" he asks, eyes still on the road.

"Not bad, thanks Dad."

There is a long pause. The rain has picked up momentum, and the wipers squeak as they go back and forth.

"Your mother and I will have been married thirty years on our anniversary, Nick," he says.

"Commiserations," I joke.

"They have been the hardest years of my life, son," he says, matter-of-factly. Then he laughs. It isn't all that often my dad makes a joke. "Only, kidding. They have definitely been the happiest."

I know that.

"I'd like to do something to celebrate. I am not very good at these sort of things, son. I was hoping that you could have a think for me, too." So there was an ulterior motive for picking me up after all, I think. I don't mind, not really. It isn't often that my dad wants to have a quiet word with me. And, for some reason, he values my opinion on the subject. My last girlfriend left me for my best mate, remember.

"I'll have a good think, Dad," I say, as we pass the turn-off for Barry.

Chapter Fifteen

How does the 'love bomb' work? – Rob Brydon

"So," she says, seductively slipping a single French fry between her lips, "what is your idea of a perfect woman, Nicholas?"

It is 2:30am Friday night/Saturday morning, on Queen Street in Cardiff. We sit at a window table of a busy burger joint. It's the quiet after the storm. We've been out on the town with work colleagues. There's been plenty of drinking and dancing and general misbehaviour. People have headed off in different directions, some of them alone (accompanied by a kebab), and some together (also accompanied by a kebab). Now there is just the two of us. All around there is madness, and yet the small table by the window, looking out on one of the busiest streets in the capital city, somehow seems completely separate from the rest of the world.

We have gradually been getting closer at work. Initially it was just little chats here and jokes there, or possibly jokes here and little chats there, whichever. But depending on the shifts people are working, you are not always guaranteed to keep the same seat from day to day, and a couple of times I've ended up sitting next to her. Yes, I don't even have my own seat. You need to get along with the person next to you otherwise the day goes too damn slow.

Sara seemed like a real mischievous chatterbox. There was never a dull moment. She asked me plenty of questions and told me a fair bit about herself, too. I once asked her how long she had been working here, and she chatted for about five minutes, telling me that it's been three years now and that although she doesn't really like it all that much, she has no idea what else to do. It is not all that bad really, though, it pays the bills and it could be worse, etc, etc. Sara continued to tell me, with great enthusiasm, that she probably won't progress because she has been pulled up too times for being cheeky with the customers. And then she clicked a button on her phone and said something along the lines of "sorry for the wait, Mr Cooper, I've managed to locate your account details now..."

"Well," I say now, deciding to take the safe, intellectual route, which I perfected in London and which I sometimes tweak now and then when making excuses to customers in work, "I strongly believe that perfection in itself is an imperfection. It is a paradox. Who would want a perfect woman, I ask you, except for an imperfect man? How boring would that be...?"

"Yeah, yeah," Sara interrupts, playfully waving a solitary finger at me, "boring! Tell me something from the heart, Nick," she challenges. She reaches forward and touches my chest. I guess that she is trying to reach my wounded, beating heart, but to be honest, I'm sure she has the wrong side. In reality I think that all she is doing is tweaking one of my nipples. "I don't want you to recite something that you read in a textbook written by an old man who has probably never even seen a woman naked before."

There is no denying that she definitely has a way with words.

I suck soda through my straw and think. Maybe the drink has made me braver than usual. This has certainly happened before, like when I've made a move on a girl on the dance floor who was just clearly, like *blatantly,* out of my league, but this feels different. It feels even braver. Right now I'm thinking about telling the truth, the whole truth and nothing but the truth.

I think of Katie and how she was the perfect girl when I was going out with her. She was slim and pretty and looked after herself and...and she was just like Suzie. And yet Suzie doesn't appeal to me at all now, even though she's a nice girl and all that. And then I remember how Katie had screwed me over, how if it was not for Katie I would still be working in London and not taking call after call in a call centre in Cardiff. I guess that might account for why I don't find Suzie all that appealing.

"Well, finding a woman you can actually trust would be a

good start. You know, like a woman who you feel would never fuck you over?"

Outside a girl in a wedding dress stumbles and then tumbles to the floor, to the amusement of her mates. There is buzzing in my ears, from the music earlier. Sara leans forward and holds my hand. "Aw, Nick," she says. "I know you've had your fingers burnt before, although I get the impression it was your pride that was hurt more than anything, if I'm honest with you, like? Do you want to talk about it?"

I'm a bit taken aback by this. I've never told her anything about Katie before.

"How do you know that?"

"I can just tell."

There is a scuffle at the front of the burger queue. Somebody's apparently tried to push in. There are raised voices and loud threats. However, it all feels like it is happening somewhere else. We are in our own little bubble. The argument is quickly broken up.

Sara really looks gorgeous tonight. I guess you take girls from work for granted. They become part of the furniture, just like the sea does when you live on the coast. Guys had been checking her out all night long. She's wearing a knee-length skirt. Her legs look shapely and toned. For some reason, though, it's her shoulders that have really raised my temperature. The narrow straps of her top barely cover the silky smooth skin.

"I do think you have to find a girl sexy, though. Otherwise you may as well go out with your best male mate."

"Is there something you want to tell me, Nick?" she asks, quizzically raising one eyebrow. "You did say that your mate Den confessed he would shag David Beckham, and you were both in your Speedos at the time in the sauna and you did tell me he had these big muscles you were jealous of, yeah?"

"No, no. Okay, I did say that, but that wasn't the point. I just mean, all that stuff about looks not being important is just not really very realistic is it, that's all."

"Do you think that the rule was made by an ugly person, Nicholas?"

"Well, definitely by somebody who has a pleasing personality rather than a handsome face, maybe somebody who has a face for radio, for example."

"But isn't beauty in the eye of the beholder, Nick?"

"Well, definitely, to a certain extent, yes. But then I'm sure that that saying was made up by an ugly person, too."

Sara giggles. She brushes her hand through her short brown hair. A stray lock falls over her eye.

"So, Nick," she says, elaborately sticking two fingers inside her mouth and sucking on them, "what sort of women do *you* find sexy?"

"Stop teasing!" I protest. "But seriously, to me, the smile is extremely important. She can have the prettiest face, the biggest boobs, but without a personality, well, it would be like shagging a blow up doll, don't you think?"

"Have you ever shagged a blow up doll then, Nicholas? How would you know, otherwise?"

"Nooo!"

"Why ever not?"

I raise both my eyes to the ceiling in apparent deep contemplation as if asking, yes, why ever not? Sara snorts and shakes her head. I look at her reflection in the dirty window and her outline is exquisite.

"Seriously, though, Nick, I really enjoy finding out what makes people tick, you know, like, by exploring under the surface and that, and I'm sure that you have more layers than most people I know."

I realise that this is a compliment, and in that way, it feels good. Straight away, though, I know that I'd almost prefer to be less complex. Life would just be so much more straightforward.

"So I am guessing that your normal route home, Nicholas, would be the train to Bridgend?"

"That would be correct."

"And what time is the last train?"

"Just before twelve."

"Hmmm. And you do realise that it is now just gone three?"

"Yes."

"So how do you plan to catch a train that left three hours ago?"

"Are you not familiar with time travel? Have you not seen *Back to the Future*?"

"No, I was washing my hair when that came on the TV," she says brushing a hand through her spiky locks.

"I will have to get a taxi," I admit.

Sara puts her hand to her mouth in mock horror. "That's going to cost a fortune!" she gasps. "Bridgend is like almost in the valleys or something? You can't get a taxi on the pittance they pay us. Besides, it's freezing out there. It's not summer, Nick."

"No choice."

Sara smiles sneakily. "Okay, here's what I suggest. If you promise to keep your hands to yourself, with no hanky-panky, you can stay at my place. I know how you like sexy girls, but really, I can't have it going around work that I'm some sort of common floozy, can I?"

She takes my hand and stands up.

"Deal."

Chapter Sixteen

I went into the attic and found a Stradivarius and a Rembrandt. Unfortunately Stradivarius was a terrible painter and Rembrandt made lousy violins – Tommy Cooper

Saturday afternoon, and I'm bored. I'm almost – *almost* – regretting not taking up my Mum's offer of strolling around the garden centre with my dad looking for hanging baskets to, well, hang in the back garden.

When I was a kid – well, about sixteen or so – I spent one dull Saturday morning ambling around in the loft. There was nothing else to do and I was sort of hoping that I might stumble on something important or valuable in there. All I remember finding, however, was an old VHS of *The Good Sex Guide*. I'm sure, looking back now with my Freudian hat on, it had an impact on me. I was not sure what scared me more – the thought that my parents had sex or the fact that they needed an instruction manual to help them.

Either way, I keep away from the attic these days, and I find myself in the back garden. It is a nice autumn day, although it's virtually winter now and truth be told, it is a little cold. I shelter my eyes from the sun with my hand. The garden looks attractive, there is no denying that. My Mum does a good job nurturing the flowers – what with her green fingers and all – and my Dad definitely keeps the lawn trimmed and tidy. In fact, there is a distinctive scent of freshly cut grass filling my senses. My eyes wander around the garden and keep coming back to one thing. I keep looking straight at the shed.

It is hidden away right in the corner of the garden. It is hardly impressive; rows of big planks of wood which have, for some reason, been painted green. The unit has no windows. It is only about ten feet by six feet or something. In conclusion, the shed is really not worthy of all the attention it receives.

The last time I went in there I was just a kid. I can't remember what I went in there for. It was just a fleeting visit, though, to dutifully tell my Dad that tea was ready or the *Antiques Roadshow* had started; something or other like that. Even then, I didn't really look inside. I popped my head through the door. Even that felt like I was intruding on my Dad's private space.

It is never locked. You can tell from outside. There are just a couple of hatches that keep it shut; one at the top, one at the bottom. My mum is extremely security conscious. The doors are always locked, even when she pops out to the garden. She never leaves her keys anywhere near the doors. She read somewhere that robbers scoop fishing lines through letterboxes and reel keys in. The image always seemed funny to me; a robber with a fishing rod. Anyway, it seems that for all the security with the house, anything goes when it comes to the shed. It is a free-for-all. There is just an unwritten rule that nobody but my Dad goes in there (I have no idea whether this unwritten rule extends to the local robbing community). Mind you, I had never been told that I *couldn't* go in there.

I remind myself of that, again and again, as I pull down the two hatches. Even then, I glance over my shoulders, just in case the neighbors can see me.

I am not sure what I am scared of, but definitely, I am scared.

It is dark inside. It is very clean and tidy. There are no cobwebs in the corners or spiders scurrying around. Everything has its place. There is no clutter. I always imagine sheds to be packed to breaking point, full of plastic plant pots, hammers and a lawn mower or two. This is not a standard shed. Dad obviously takes pride in the place.

I take a closer inspection.

There is a tall (it must be five feet or so) wooden filing cabinet standing prominently in one corner, and a black and white plastic cupboard in the other. I open the cupboard. There are little glass tubs and pots of paint and palate plates stored carefully inside. I feel relieved and disappointed. It is evident that my Dad has been using the shed for painting after all. He is just boring old Dad, who potters around inside the shed.

I think about just leaving. I tip-toe back and forth. I slowly and carefully pull out the top tray from the wooden filing cabinet, making sure that I don't damage anything.

I remove a sheet of brown paper. A canvas rests underneath a transparent, thin sheet of glass. Lying underneath, a painting depicts the cliffs of Southerndown at sunset. The fading orange sun contrasts beautifully with the dark blue of the sea. The steeply sloping cliff casts a shadow over the rocks and pebbles on the shore.

I'm even more carful now. I pat the brown paper down and straighten it out. I push the tray back into the cabinet before pulling open the second tray. Again, I remove the delicate sheet of brown paper. The setting is instantly recognizable: the sand dunes at Merthyr Mawr. I can almost hear the gentle flowing of the stream just to the front of the car park, always sheltered by the overhanging trees.

I make sure I leave everything just as I found it. Anything else would be just unbearably disrespectful. I shut the door and pull the two hatches back into position and return to the patio and the sun shining brightly against into my face. It doesn't seem boring now; just peaceful and relaxing. I could quite contentedly sit here all afternoon.

I guess I didn't really find anything in the shed. My father does just spend his time in there painting, after all. But I know that is not quite right. Just like most people, I really know nothing about painting, apart from what I like.

And I really, really liked my dad's paintings.

And somehow, that feels important.

Chapter Seventeen

Words impress me. If a man can speak eloquently and beautifully to me, I just melt on the floor- Catherine Zeta Jones

Wednesday night at ten and I'm lying on my bed, legs in the air, feet pressed firmly against the wall. There is a hole in one of my socks. I'm contemplating whether or not to just go to sleep. I've been like this for ninety minutes now.

I had my one-to-one at work with Pam just before lunch. It went well. I've completely transformed my sales figures. I'm topping the whole team, Pam said. I was feeling pretty pleased with myself, to be honest. I was still working in a call centre, but at least I was now doing my job well working in a call centre. It was a small victory, but a victory, nevertheless.

When I came home, my mum was furiously cleaning. In fact, she was in her cleaning gear; trainers, tee-shirt and navy tracksuit bottoms. I tip-toed into the lounge, making sure that I didn't put my feet on the settee, that I didn't do anything at all that could make me accused of 'making the place look untidy.'

"What time do you want tea?" my mum asked. She stood in the middle of the room, her yellow rubber gloves on, hands on hips.

This felt like a trick question. I chose my words as if they were my very last ones. "Whatever time is good for you, Mum," I said, smiling.

This response wasn't to her satisfaction, however. She jerked her head from side to side and stormed out of the room. "Really," she shouted to me from the hallway, "I'm quite sure that you are perfectly capable of cooking food every so often yourself, Nicholas!"

It was difficult to relax when she was in this mood. In fact, it completely affected my viewing enjoyment of *Come Dine with Me*. Her feet stomped back into the living room and again she stood in the middle of the room, hands on hips. The rubber gloves, though, had now been removed.

"I thought you would be busy looking for another job now, Nick?"

Doubtless, she didn't really think I would be busy right now looking for another job, because these days I am absolutely never busy looking for another job.

"I'm just watching *Come Dine with Me,* Mum," I offered, timidly.

"Oh, that's okay then, darling. Obviously *Come Dine with Me* comes ahead of your career and your future in general, doesn't it, Nick? It's not as if you do any cooking around here, anyway!"

I sensed sarcasm. Whatever I said next would be shot down. So, I just didn't say anything. I looked at her in silence, probably pretty gormlessly.

"You told your dad and me that you were just taking this job as an interim, darling, and that you would be looking for another job at the same time. Your father is ever so worried about you, Nick. I really don't think you worked so hard in University to work in a call centre, do you?"

It had honestly, genuinely, been my intention just to accept the job for the interim. They (whoever they are) tell you that it is easier to find another job when you are already working, that you are more appealing to employers and there is less pressure on you etc, etc (blah-de-blah). Yet they do not take into consideration that fact that, after a day at work, you are usually too exhausted to look for the remote control, let alone look for another job.

"Don't worry, Mum. I'll crack on with it tonight."

We both knew that that, just like the obsessive cleaning, my employment status was a sub-issue, a distraction from the real concerns that were playing on her mind. Nan was still in hospital, although hopefully not for too much longer, and it was tearing Mum apart not being there with her.

And so, straight after a silent dinner, I locked myself in my room, and I've just been contentedly lying her ever since.

The phone vibrates.

"Hello."

"Hello, handsome."

"Oh, hello, Sara, how are you?" I press my feet harder against the wall.

"I'm good, thanks. What are you up to?"

"I m just lying here on my bed; I'm not doing anything at all, really."

"Were you masturbating, Nicholas?" Sarah asks, lowering her voice.

"No!" I protest, lowering my feet and sitting upright. "Just because somebody is lying on their bed without sleeping, it doesn't mean that they have to be you-know-what, you know."

"Doesn't it? Speak for yourself, handsome." There is a deep, mischievous chuckle down the receiver.

"Anyway, I was just wondering why you didn't make a move on me when you stayed at my house, Nick."

I'm used to Sara's straight talking; in fact, it's one of the things that I like about her.

"You told me not to?"

"Well, obviously I did. But that doesn't mean I don't want you to."

"Oh, right."

"I was thinking one of two things, Nick," Sara says.

"Oh right," I say, again. "What are those two things then?" I can hear steps on the stairs, and hide my face under the covers to muffle my voice.

"Well, you mentioned going out with a best male friend. So, are you gay?"

"No!" I protest, my voice high-pitched.

"Okay," Sara says, seeming to accept this. I don't think it was really a serious question, anyway. "You also mentioned that you need to find a girl sexy. So do you not find me sexy, Nick?"

"No!" I exclaim, hurriedly. "No, I mean, no, it's not that. I mean, yes, I do find you sexy. I find you very sexy, Sara…"

There is a brief pause on the other end of the phone. "That's nice to know, Nicholas. So what was the problem, then?"

Now this was a good question. I didn't really know the

answer myself. Okay, I was scared, but I then I wasn't exactly sure why I was scared.

"There's no problem at all, Sara, I promise," I say. I pull the bed sheets from over my head. I decide to be brave. I am not brave all that often and so in a way I was being brave just by deciding to be brave.

"In fact," I continue, my voice breaking slightly, "I was going to ask you if you would like to accompany me somewhere on Saturday, Sara…"

***

"So, Nicholas, honestly now; have you ever been caught bashing the old bishop?"

I'm amazed by the apparent innocence of the question. Sara may as well be asking whether I've added extra sugar to an already sugary bowl of *Frosties.*

"That's a bit of a 'wank' question, isn't it?" I retort, just like that.

We are on the A48, just outside Bridgend, heading towards Cardiff. It is raining heavily outside and Sara has been struggling to clear the windscreen. Subsequently, it's absolutely boiling inside the car. We pass a bag of potatoes on the side of the road with a sign next to it saying potatoes are for sale. I've passed that bag of potatoes quite a few times since I've been back in Bridgend. I wonder whether anyone has ever passed and thought that's just what is missing from my life, a big bag of potatoes. One day I am going to buy some, just because.

"You remind me of Michael Parkinson," I tell her, "what with all these questions and all."

"What, I remind you of a man?" she asks.

"No," I protest. "I mean, like a chat show host."

She does not look convinced, or maybe she is just concentrating on the road. She wrinkles her cute little nose and asks me to clarify my response to her initial question.

I tell her that, contrary to popular belief, I have never been much of a 'wanker'. My father never gave me a 'birds and the bees' speech, which was probably for the best, because I think it may have set off a heart attack, and so I was unusually innocent and naïve about all things sexual. I always felt guilty about doing it, blissfully unaware that my mates were probably at it morning, noon and night. I never knew much until I picked up bits and bobs from my mates, I told her.

"So who was this bloke Bob you picked up?" Sara asks.

I've noticed she is very sharp like that. You can make a big speech and she will pick out a single word, maybe the most trivial part of what you have said, and make that the focal point.

"There was this one time…" I say, just leaving it there, waiting for her to bite.

Sara seems happy enough not to bite.

"Don't you want to know more?" I eventually ask.

"Sorry, Nick, I was just trying to annoy you, because it was pretty obvious you were waiting for me to ask."

"Okay, fair enough. Anyway, I was at my nan's house. I was about fourteen. It was a really hot afternoon. My dad was there with my nan in the back garden, mowing the lawn, which is what he tends to do when he is at her house, even when the lawn really does not need mowing…"

"Is that part relevant?" Sara asks, hands firmly on the steering wheel, eyes still focussed on the road.

"Not really."

"Okay, continue…"

"Anyway, I am sat on her old brown sofa in the lounge reading the paper. I'm wearing a pair of shorts, because it's so hot. I'm looking at the Page Three girl in the paper. Without thinking, really, I slipped a hand inside my shorts and started playing, like. Next thing I know my nan is looking through the window, telling me that I should come outside because it's such a nice day. I stop what I'm doing, and she notices what I'm doing, and I'll be honest, there were a few awkward moments when my nan was staring at me with my cock in my hand."

Sara starts laughing, and it's such a loud, wonderful cackle. "So in a nutshell, Nick, bypassing the unnecessary lawn mowing stuff, you are saying that your nan caught you wanking in her house, in the middle of the day, on her sofa, in her living room?"

I'm blushing, and it's partly because of the unbearable heat and partly through embarrassment. "Well," I say, "when you put it like that, I guess it doesn't sound too good."

"So what were you like as a child, Nick?" Sara asks. I notice that she is surprisingly quite a good driver. I'm not sure why this is a surprise. She has programmed in the post code I have given her, and she is following the navigation provided by the lady with the posh voice.

"Up till about the age of say six I'd say that I was an exceptionally stupid child," I say, with complete honesty.

Sara nods her head. She doesn't look surprised at all. "In what way?" she asks.

"Well, my mum says that I never said much. I had to go to speech therapy because even the words I did say came out all wrong. And when I started school, I really didn't have a clue what was going on. My teacher would pull on my ears because I just wouldn't listen to anything she said. But truth is; it wasn't that I didn't listen, I just didn't have a clue what she was going on about."

"Awww, you poor thing," Sara says, all sincerely, patting my leg.

"But then when I got to about six it all seemed to click. My mum read me stories all the time and she tried to get me to read, but I just couldn't. But then, I don't know, I just could read, and better than most of the other kids in my class, too."

"So you have a lot to thank your mother for then? It sounds like she really put in the work to help you," Sara says.

I'd never thought about it before, but I know that she is right, a bit begrudgingly.

"I always had a very curious mind though," I say, proudly. "I was always fascinated by things. I remember this one time I was with my nan and she had to deliver something to a neighbour. Anyway, this neighbour had a white wooden gate. Now, most children my age would have just seen it as a white gate, but not me. I wanted to see whether I could fit my head between the gaps in the wooden panels. As I said, I had a curious mind."

"And could you?"

"Yes, it was an extremely tight fit, but I managed to squeeze my head in. They couldn't get my head out, though, and I was stuck there for about an hour before the owners of the gate decided enough was enough and they cut one of the panels off with a saw."

"And you are proud of this story, Nick?" Sara asks. "This is an example of your curious mind?"

I realise that she has a point and just timidly nod my head.

"So we are here, Nick," Sara announces, pulling the car into an empty, drab car park. "Where is it exactly that you are taking me?"

I feel nervous. I question whether this has all been a mistake. We are in a quiet part of Penarth on a wet Saturday morning and Sara must be thinking there are better things to be doing on her weekend off. But it is too late now. I go to the boot and pull out the items and then take Sara's hand and tentatively walk to the shop just across the road.

A bell rings when the door opens. I think it is possibly an indication that they do not get many customers. It smells of damp carpet. The shop is dimly lit. A man with a black beard with specks of grey and stooped shoulders appears from out the back and asks if he can help.

I pull open the black bin bag and ask whether he could please value the item.

The man adjusts his glasses, which rest precariously on the tip of his nose. He carefully rests the painting against the counter. Sara is busy browsing around the shop. It really is full – cluttered even – with paintings and ornaments and statues, and she 'coos' and 'ahhs' and comments that they are all so beautiful. Unlike my dad's shed, things do not seem to have their place. The man examines the first painting that I came across; the one of Southerndown at sunset.

I'm really nervous. It would hurt me if the man dismissed the painting, said that it was a load of rubbish.

He seems to be taking his time though.

"Do you know who the artist is?"

It is funny hearing that word 'artist' and I stifle a laugh. I tell him that it is just a family member, not a known artist.

He looks at me now, and I notice that, hidden away behind his glasses, one of his eyes is not quite right. I'm sure it is a glass eye. I concentrate on the other eye.

"Well, it's a very good piece of work. The attention to detail and the contrast of colours is quite something, very impressive. I'll give you fifty pounds for it, and that's a good price. I would not consider any more for an unrecognised artist, but I do like to help new painters."

"Oh, I don't want to sell it!" I exclaim, high-pitched. Realising that the man is looking at me strangely, with his one eye, I quickly continue, "what I mean is, I will need to check with the artist that he is happy with that price."

The man nods his head and smiles and says, "well, you know where I am." He seems happy enough. I wouldn't want to upset him, not after he has done me a favour and been respectful about it, too. My mind is all over the place, though, and I want to get out of here. I take Sara's hand, and she seems reluctant to leave, but she follows me out and the bell rings again as we leave.

It's raining even heavier than before outside, and puddles are everywhere.

"Quick," I say, squeezing Sara's hand tighter, and lead her inside a café just two doors down.

We sit down by the window sipping hot chocolate from enormous mugs. We do not say anything, but it feels nice. The window is steamed up. Sara's normally pale cheeks look flushed and damp from the rain. I'm surprised, as I always am, by how pretty she is.

I think about the shop. The owner of the shop said that it was an impressive piece of work. He gave me a good price, and he needs to make a profit on that, too. I don't know what I think now.

"Was your dad the artist, Nick?" Sarah eventually asks.

"How did you know?"

"It just makes sense."

I nod my head. I had told her about my dad pottering around in the shed; that he does a bit of painting in there. I am always prone to exaggeration, though. She probably thinks that my parents are a couple of loonies.

"So what are you going to do now?" she asks.

"What do you mean?"

"Now that you know he's actually a good painter?"

I ponder this for a moment. "I really have no idea," I tell her truthfully.

Sara reaches forward and takes my hand.

"Thanks so much for bringing me today, Nick," she says. And then we sit in silence again until we have both finished our drinks.

Chapter Eighteen

When one burns ones bridges, what a nice fire it makes – Dylan Thomas

London

The Liberty Club, smack bang in the heart of the West End, is in full flow. It is Friday and it's just gone one in the morning and the whole world according to Paul Richards is totally and utterly fantastic.

Paul is out with Matt and John, two friends from his schooldays in Dagenham. Paul has to admit that his two friends are doing pretty well for themselves nowadays. Matt is a mechanic for a Mercedes dealership, while John runs his own plumbing business. They still look up to him, though, just like they did in school. They don't have a clue what he does, not really; but they know he works in the city, which means that he never, ever has to get his hands dirty.

They lean against the bar. Matt has just got another round of shots in. Glasses are clinked together and shots are quickly drained. Paul squeezes his eyes shut and grimaces. His two single friends, he observes, are not exactly likely to be enticing the ladies tonight. Matt has not bothered to clean his finger nails of the grease and grime that he's accumulated through hard, physical days fixing the rich man's motor. John has a perfectly round little pot belly that protrudes proudly over his low-hanging jeans. One of the buttons on his red and black lumberjack shirt is undone, and pale unhealthy flesh is visible through the hole. But then, attracting women doesn't appear to be on their radar; not tonight, not any night, for that matter. His two mates seem content on getting hammered and stopping off for a kebab on the way home. Where's their ambition? Paul is already thinking about losing them when the perfect opportunity presents itself.

John picks up a half-empty pint from the adjacent table.

It's not his drink. He's so far gone though, Paul thinks, he probably imagines that every drink is his drink. He pulls the pint to his mouth and, holding onto the bar for support, drains the glass in one. A guy stands right in his face, his chest pumped out; trying his best to look menacing. A couple of mates are quickly on their feet, backing the man up. John isn't bothered by the numbers, though. He could take on the whole Goddamn club if he needed to tonight. He presses the palm of his hand in the man's face and pushes him away. The man bounces back, like he is attached to a spring. It's all about to kick off. The bouncers wade in to break up the melee. John kicks and flails his legs wildly as he is bundled out of the fire exit. Matt follows behind, angrily stabbing his middle finger in the direction of the security, but it's all to show face, just so that they can tell the story to their mates down the pub the next afternoon, nursing warm beers.

Paul, however, takes a different direction. He disappears within a sliver of space in the dance floor, dissolving into a tiny dot, absorbed by hundreds or thousands of other tiny dots. He knows that his two friends will be outside in the cold, already eying up the flashing lights of the kebab house, their stomachs rumbling and their heads nipping. They will not even realise that he is not there with them until it is too late, and even then they will assume that he got caught up in it and they separated. These things happen.

Paul is on top of the world now. He is free. The music pumps through the club in the same way that the adrenaline pumps through his body. His friends are a distant memory. They never even existed. The dance floor and the music are his new friends, but then his best buddy in the whole world right now, the only friend that really counts, is the cocaine he snorted in the toilets about fifteen or so minutes ago.

Paul looks good, he knows that. He gazes around and feels like the centre of the universe. All that working out at home, he thinks, toning his body to the fitness channels on the TV, have made him the best looking guy in the whole club, in the whole of London.

He flashes a smile at a girl, any girl, on the floor around him. The girl smiles back. Paul does not hesitate. He makes his move, edging closer, his body twisting and gyrating. His hands rest on her narrow hips, slide behind the curve of her back. Paul nestles his face against her cheek. She has an odour of strong perfume blended with fresh, sweet, sugary sweat. He whispers in her ear; says that she is the most beautiful girl in the club, in the whole world. The girl laughs delightedly. She whispers in his ear now; says that he is the most handsome man in the club, in the whole world.

Paul doesn't want this party to end.

There is a whole group of them in a big taxi now, heading back to a flat where the party will continue. Paul thinks that they are heading to Tooting Bec or maybe it is Tooting Broadway, one or the other for sure, but then again, it might not be either. It does not matter where they are going so long as the party does not end. The bright green digits of the digital clock on the dashboard of the taxi say that it is three o'clock. The rest of the world will be sleeping now. It is a weekday, and so there will be work tomorrow. The sleepers will be getting up in three or so hours. Thank God, Paul thinks, that he doesn't have any work tomorrow.

Paul is introduced to everyone in the taxi and he shakes their hands and smiles and tells them that he is Paul, a friend of Becky, that even though he's only just met her, they feel a real connection. The occupants of the taxi nod their heads slowly, as if they know exactly what he means.

Back at the flat they all sit in a circle, legs crossed, drinking and smoking and talking about the economy and politics, or maybe it is religion and the environment. It does not matter to Paul. He is their willing disciple. Everything they say sounds so wise and rational.

And then, just like that, the colours in the room fade and everything is dark and black and grey.

Paul uncrosses his legs and stretches them out but that does not feel right either and he starts fidgeting and twisting. He has a compulsion to press the flat of his foot against the floor. His nose is running, or maybe it is bleeding, and he wipes it with his sleeve. The sound of the whining voices is making him tired. It all sounds like noise. He tries to pass the time by necking Becky, however her mouth tastes like she has just swallowed a bottle of cod liver oil tablets, and she does not look so angelic any more, either. He notices small red spots on her chin and there are cracks in her chalky foundation. The girl that he thought so beautiful in the darkness of the club appals him now, and he longs to push her away. Light seeps through a crack in the curtain. Paul feels a searing pain right in the centre of his forehead.

It is time for some more cocaine. He departs to the toilet and locks the door.

Paul puts his hand in one pocket and then his other hand in the other pocket. He pulls the pockets inside out; starts panicking. It isn't there. It must be there. It isn't there. It just *has* to be there. It still isn't there.

It must have fallen out of his pocket, Paul concludes. He tries to re trace his steps - that's what everyone would tell him to do, ask him what he did last, what he has been doing - but there are so many steps and he has be doing so much. It could have fallen in the club, it could have been in the taxi, it could have been anywhere, but all he knows is, it isn't here, where it should be, where it absolutely needs to be. Nothing else matters right now but that little bag of beautiful white coke. He can deal with anything that happens tomorrow or the day after that but right now all he needs is just a tiny little bit of coke, just enough to get him through this devastating black low.

Sweat seeps through his shirt. He knows that this small enclosed toilet reeks of stale body odour; *his* body odour. Paul stares at his reflection in the small cracked mirror on the wall and realises that he doesn't look anywhere as good as he thought he did, or as good as he always used to. His skin looks dull and oily and there is a faint but noticeable white outline inside his nostrils. He knows can be mended or at least hidden with some soap and water and a towel. His eyes are what frighten him the most. He pushes his face close to the mirror now, so that all that stares back at him are his dilating pupils. The look in those eyes cannot be mended or hidden.

Paul clicks the lock and wanders out into the kitchen and stands against the side of the sink. He cannot stop sweating, it is everywhere. He needs to be somewhere different, but he still needs to be somewhere alone. Paul cannot be seen, not looking like this, without a mask or camouflage.

It becomes apparent, however, that Paul is not alone. One of the faces from the taxi (they all looked pretty much the same, but this one had a monstrous, unkempt beard), is staring at him. The face is not friendly, not like it was in the taxi. The face with the beard looks angry. The narrow slit of a mouth is talking to Paul, asking questions and demanding answers. The man wants to know what Paul is doing with Becky, says something about her being his. Paul tries to remember who Becky is but his mind is foggy and instead he wonders whether this man might have some cocaine on him. He does not know what the man is talking about but he sounds angry but if he has coke then he will be his best friend in the whole world. The man keeps on shouting at him, however, and Paul knows that he doesn't have any coke and now he really, really just wants him to go away, to please, please go away.

Paul waves his trembling hand dismissively, says that he can have Becky, that he doesn't even want her; that her mouth smells real bad. But the man doesn't seem to like this, the information doesn't translate well, and he picks up a knife from the sink and lunges at him. Paul can only react through instinct. This man is trying to hurt him and he needs to stop this from happening. He lashes out with his foot and kicks the man, just to keep him away. However, he connects firmly with the groin. The man keels forward and whimpers pathetically. The knife drops to the floor. Paul swings with his clenched left fist and feels his knuckle connect against bone.

There is mayhem and madness now. The other partygoers rush into the room, asking him what happened, what he did, what his problem is. One of the girls screams. His skull is throbbing. It feels like it is going to explode. Paul needs to get out of here, like now. He tries to speak but he doesn't know what to say, he doesn't have any answers and the words just will not come out in the right order. His hands just will not say still. Paul steps over the man, lying immobile and silent on the floor, and moves towards the door. A single hand reaches out, calling him back, begging him to stay. He knows the hand belongs to the most beautiful girl in the club – she may have been the one for him - but that felt so long ago now, like a different lifetime, and it is never going to happen now.

Paul climbs down the stairs and slams the door behind him. He wants to sit down. His legs cannot cope, nor his lungs. He finds a bench in a park just down the road. It is now daylight. Men in suits with deadlines and a purpose walk along the path towards the tube station. Children with satchels and an education and a future with such simple lives stare at him uncaringly. Paul wonders whether they think he is a tramp. He bows his head and covers his eyes from the blinding, painful sun with his hands.

Paul knows that this party has well and truly ended, and not just for tonight, either.

Although he knows he probably looks more desolate than ever, sat alone on the bench, Paul feels better than he did. His thinking is clearer, more realistic, and not distorted by fantasy. Paul knows that he hasn't told Matt and John, his closest friends from school, that he hasn't been to work for months, but then he hasn't told anyone. His life as they know it is just an illusion. He has been wearing a mask for a long time now. This is the real Paul, sat on a park bench in the early hours of the morning whilst everyone else is going to work or school.

He is still paid by *360 Ltd*, but Paul knows that this is not through choice. They are merely going through the formalities, covering the red tape. He is no longer the favourite of the big boss man, Max Vaughan, like he once was, a long, long time ago, when Nick was just his side-kick.

Paul only ever intended to take a few days off, maybe a week at most, but then a week turned into two and then a month and now the thought of going back to work brings such an incredible feeling of crippling anxiety that he has no idea how he will ever return.

He often wonders how it happened, but he still struggles for a definitive answer. It was never his grand plan; he just slipped and kept on sliding. He'd always been aware that he was easily bored and never satisfied. Even securing the next big deal or pulling the hottest girl in the club wasn't enough anymore. It was all superficial. The first time he tried the cocaine, however, it felt real. Just for a few, perfect moments, it gave him a sublime high. He didn't need to search for the next big deal or chase the next hottest girl. This was the only high he needed. For those few, perfect moments, Paul Richards was content.

Of course, the high was more addictive than any he'd experienced before. He was like a vampire seeking blood. As soon as the high faded, everything became bleaker than ever. Before, the world bored him. Now, without the coke, it became unbearable. He needed it just to keep going, just to remain on a level.

He was already going downhill when the whole Nick thing happened. Paul wasn't sure what he was thinking, but he sure knew that he wasn't thinking straight. He really liked Nick, but that was part of the problem. Nick had always looked up to him, Paul was sure of that. But whereas he was slipping, Nick was only getting more confident, more skilled. He was overtaking him. And Nick seemed to have pretty much everything sorted, too. He acted like he was a pleasure seeker, but all he really wanted in life was a decent job, a woman who loved him, and a happy, healthy family. He didn't have the thirst for sensational highs and lows. Paul was sure that Nick could cope with him getting a major one over on him. Katie wasn't the right girl for him anyway. She was a shallow spoilt little bitch who only cared about herself and what other people thought of her. Nick was better shot of her. He was doing him a favour really.

However much he tried to justify it in his mind, it just didn't work.

The next morning he woke in her bed and sobbed like a baby. All he felt was loathing, not for Nick, who he really loved, or for Katie, who he just didn't care about, but for himself.

Paul rises to his feet and walks unsteadily towards the tube station. He wonders what Nick is doing now. He heard that he is back in Wales. He hopes that he is doing okay, that he is getting on with his life.

Paul tells himself, again and again, as he sees the sign for the tube station in the distance, if he can just make it home, that if he can make it to his duvet, where he can hide away from the rest of the world, then he might just make it through another day.

Chapter Nineteen

Don't worry about a thing, every little thing is gonna to be alright – Bob Marley

It's Sunday evening at about four o'clock, and Den and I have met up in town. We sit on a low wall, our backs pressing against icy black railings, and look out at the main road running through the town centre. Autumn has turned to winter. There is a light drizzle of snow in the air, but earlier it was snowing heavily and so our feet sink into the crunchy, delicious layer that covers the pavement. The tips of the trees are sprinkled white, like icing on a cake. I ponder for a moment all the pain and inconvenience the snow will cause in the coming days, but looking out now at the distant fields glistening and proud, all I can think is how beautiful it is.

Den is somewhere underneath all the clothes. When I was a little kid, my mum never used to let me leave the house in the winter unless my coat was zipped right to the top and I put on a matching bobble hats and mitts, but you can tell that with Den his mum never had to bother. With his hood pulled down low so it looks like he has no forehead, he is the first black Eskimo in Bridgend. Still, he shivers and bounces up and down on the spot and elaborately blows steam from his mouth.

"It can't be that cold, Den," I say helpfully, trying to reassure him that it's all in his mind. "Remember, if it's too cold, it won't snow."

He slowly moves his head towards me, like his neck is in plaster or something. The look on his face is a mixture of pity and disdain.

"If it wasn't fucking cold then it wouldn't be snowing at all," he spits.

He had called me early afternoon and asked if I fancied popping into town later. I was a bit surprised because I pictured him sat by a fire somewhere drinking hot chocolate and eating marshmallows, but it was just a lazy Sunday afternoon and so I said sure, why not. I assumed that we would be frequenting some of the local public houses, but when I met him at the bus station, Den already had a six pack in a white plastic bag and said that he just fancied hanging out like we used to in the old days. I remember thinking that the only reason we hung out in parks and bus shelters and in the church when we were teenagers was because nobody would let us into the pubs, but Den had already bought the cans, and so who was I to argue?

"Once we've finished these," Den says now, warming his cheeks with the flat of his gloves, "do you fancy going to a few pubs? We might be able to find a few pieces of fluff that need warming up."

I smile to myself. This is more like the old Den.

"Anyway, talking of pieces of fluff, I picked up this tidy bird the other night, and before I knew it, her tits were out, her fanny was wet and I was going down on her…"

That's not like you, Den, I think.

"We were back at her place, you know, and to be honest she was starting to bore me a bit, which is quite unusual when the girl in question is freely bouncing up and down on my substantial manhood, I can tell you. The thing is, every time she did anything, and I mean anything, she'd ask if she was being naughty. She took off her bra and she was like 'ooh, am I naughty?' She went down south and she was like 'ooh, am I naughty?' She stuck a finger up her…"

Den makes me laugh. One moment he seems glum, the next there is a wicked smile on his face.

"But that really is veering away from the point of my story. After I'd delivered her to heaven and back, and then back again, this woman looked at her watch, and after asking if she was naughty said 'ooh, I hope my husband doesn't come home any time soon…"

"Husband?"

"Yeah, that's what I said, too! She was like, yeah, well who do you think the man is in all those photographs? And I was like, I don't know, love, I was too busy unfastening your bra to look at any photographs…"

"Those straps can be tricky, can't they?"

"Yeah, well anyway Nick, this is where we get to the point. This woman jumps off me, and she was quite high up, if you know what I'm saying, big man, and she says something along the lines of 'don't worry about it, butt, it's all harmless good fun, isn't it? Just a bit of banter, like?"

Oh, Den was right. This *was* interesting. He nods his head now as if in acknowledgement of the point.

The thing is; we had worked hard to produce a concrete and universal definition of 'banter.' It had begun with Sam, in our final year at school. He spent a whole double semester in the library nurturing and perfecting a definition. The thing with Sam, though, is that he liked to use ten words when one would have sufficed. Den was the opposite. If he could get away with it, he wouldn't use any words at all. Sam's definition, therefore, was long-winded and technical. In a nutshell, though, it basically stated that 'banter' was the allowance for one party to give unlimited abuse to another party because there was a mutual understanding that no genuine offence was intended.

However, this previously insignificant oh-aren't-I-naughty-married-woman had blown this definition out of the water, and caused quite a stir in the process, because her version of the term had no relevance at all to either abuse or offence, intended or not.

I think about this for a moment.

"I'm suggesting that we either need to review our definition or dismiss her use as inappropriate?" I say.

Den nods his head. "That is what I thought," he says. "However, I decided that in order to reach either conclusion we'd have to do some serious thinking first, yes?"

High-five. God, I think, sometimes my friend can be smart.

I roll some snow from the wall and mould it into a perfect ball, conscious to avoid the imperfections in the perfect white, the patches where the snow has faded yellow or brown. A couple of kids walk past on the other side of the pavement, all kitted out in their best winter gear. They can't be any more than ten or so, and they excitedly talk about sledging down the dunes if they are off school tomorrow. I nudge Den on the arm and then cheekily launch the ball in their direction. It rises and dips and then splatters over the smallest boy's head.

"Cheeky fuckers!" the little kid screams (a tad inappropriately), but he soon shrugs it off and sees the funny side when his mates start laughing.

Den proper chuckles at this and so I immediately roll up another ball and throw it at the next unsuspecting passers-by, a couple in their twenties. This time I misfire and my snow ball crashes against the concrete wall in front of them. They are an easy-going couple seemingly in good spirits and the woman turns and says something about it being lucky that I fire blanks.

I roll up my next ball (and I'll be honest, they seem to be getting progressively bigger), and hand it to Den.

"Your turn."

He does not seem so keen, and sheepishly puts his hands back in his pockets. "Nah, man," he mutters. "I'll probably hurt someone, the power I get in my throws."

I remember from school that Den throws like a girl, but I humour him, nevertheless. "Just throw it more gently then, Den," I encourage him, trying to remove any trace of sarcasm from my voice.

Den reluctantly takes the ball and carelessly lobs it at the next couple that come along, however he slips and the ball veers wayward to the left, and it crashes against the shoulder of a lady who must be in her seventies, who is walking arm in arm with her husband.

Den runs out across the road with his hands raised to his chest, apologising madly, saying that he meant to hit the couple in front. Only, he is wearing shoes that have a narrow tip and no grip whatsoever and he slides like Bambi on ice, one leg going left and the other going right until he is doing the splits and screaming high-pitched in the middle of the road. The elderly couple don't know what to make of all of this and they look at Den confused for a moment or two before the husband utters "just be careful what you are doing with those balls of yours, young man," and they continue with their walk.

I'm laughing hysterically as Den returns to our side of the road, his head now bowed to the floor and his steps slow and unsteady.

"Eh, Dennard, what you thinking you doing, throwing snowballs at old people? Oh my days!"

I know instantly who it is.

"Mum?" Den says, and I'm sure that he blushes. "I didn't see you there, Mum. What you doing here?"

It put my hand over my mouth to stop my hysterics, but still it's no good, and I cough loudly, spluttering and sniffing like I have the wickedest of colds, bordering on man flu. Den's mum looks at him now, her hands on her ample hips, staring open-mouth, completely aghast. She too is wrapped up in layers and layers, but still she looks immaculate, as she always does, her hair sitting in a perfect bun, and her lipstick matching (it cannot be deliberate, surely?) her purple woollen cashmere. The black boots are knee length and perfectly practical for this weather, and yet not compromising one iota on style.

"Me?" Mrs Jones asks, digging a pointed, manicured finger into her chest. "Where do you think I'm going? It is Sunday, so church, no? Your father is working late again, tut. Again it is just me to go church on my own. So what *you* doing, Dennard?"

My big friend Den, with all his swagger and muscles, is like a mouse. He starts rambling, telling her how he was just having a bit of fun with Nick when oh-my-God it was ever so funny, he slipped and accidentally hit an old lady and then slipped again and anyway we all laughed and no harm done really, Mum. Mrs Jones raises her eyebrows and keeps on raising them until they join the faint creases on her forehead. It is as if Den has picked up a shovel and just keeps on digging and digging. Mrs Jones does not look impressed, not one bit.

"What is this?" she asks, holding the palms of her hands out by her side. "Is this the sort of behaviour that your father and I brought up? Eh?" She points her finger accusingly at Den, who lowers his eyes to the floor. I've seen Mrs Jones seemingly very angry and very loud many times before, and yet she always gives the impression that she will break into a smile at any moment, as though it's all in jest, really, even when, sometimes, its not.

She seems to notice me for the first time, even though Den has been talking about me, and her mood changes, just like that.

"Ah, Nick!" she says, giving me a kiss on the cheek and a big hug before breaking into a gorgeous smile. "Can you not keep my boy out of trouble?" she laughs, clearing her throat and shaking her head from side to side.

"I hear you got a job in Cardiff," she continues. "Well done. These jobs are hard to come by now. Very well done, you," and she squeezes my hand before turning to Den and saying, "this one – he does no work at all. Nan in Jamaica is so worried about him. She says to me, 'that Den, what is wrong with him? Is he ill?' You know? He does not go to school; he does not go to work. His father, he went to school first and then went to work. His brother Patrick, he goes to work every day in a suit. It is just this one."

I love Den's mum, and I always have. She's a bright light, funny and kind, and she'd do absolutely anything for her family. Whenever I've been to her house, she's always treated me like a king, feasting me with mountains of food and an endless supply of drink. Den's dad has done well for himself, so it seems, gaining qualifications in accounts, and he works long hours and earns the money for the house. He comes home and everything is done for him, and I get the impression that's just the way it's supposed to be.

She calls it how it is however, and she does give Den a hard time. Right now I don't know where to look, because I'm starting to feel bad for him. Den is silent. He wouldn't even think of answering back to his mum. I've seen him fight back against some of the toughest guys in town, but never, ever his mum.

The only time I've known Mrs Jones glow with pride is when Den was working. I was the only one who went to University as it turned out. Sam had a place all sorted in London and he had plenty of other offers, too, but he went missing the day we got our exam results, and Den failed his

A-Levels and got a job in a bank in town instead. He started on a real poor wage, by all accounts, but he was only nineteen and he seemed to be doing really well. Guess you could say he slipped in shit and still came out smelling of roses. I remember going to his house and Mrs Jones referring to him as 'my little worker,' and putting her arm around him. But he lost his job and as far I'm aware, he hasn't worked since. And Den has been in prison since. I doubt, thinking about it, that Mrs Jones has been proud of Den for quite some time.

"Den will be alright, Mrs Jones, I promise you," is all I can think of saying.

She nods her head and quietly mutters that she hopes so.

"Nick, why have you not been around our house for food? Why is this?" she asks.

There is always a plentiful supply of food at the Jones's house. I don't know if it is a cultural thing, but the family take pride in how lavishly they treat their guests. Mrs Jones's food is always delicious, too; full of taste and spices and colour. I remember this one time I ate like I had a shovel in my hand and finished before Den and Patrick had even made a dent in their food. I was full to bursting, like I'd just finished Christmas lunch or something. I couldn't face another mouthful. Mrs Jones saw my empty plate and chuckled. "Nick, you need some more!" she exclaimed. It was an order, and not a question. She clinked around in the pots and pans, but the food had all gone. Mrs Jones was not to be beaten, though. She couldn't possibly leave her guest wanting more food, not in her house, no. I could see her racking her mind for an alternative. She found one, in the end. She picked up Patrick's plate and scooped the remains of his food onto mine. "There you go! You have plenty of food now, Nick! Eat up!" she said. I will always remember the bemused look on Patrick's face when he realised that I was eating his dinner.

"What time is church, Mrs Jones?" I ask.

"Started fifteen minutes ago," she answers. "So I'm making good time," and she laughs again, and it really is a lovely, gorgeous laugh.

She gives me a kiss and then she gives Den a kiss and a hug, and he hugs her back, and she walks off in the direction of the church.

We don't speak for a while. I guess we are both deep in thought. Maybe Den doesn't know what to say either.

Eventually Den blows more steam from his mouth and says "pub?"

And he doesn't even wait for my response.

Chapter Twenty

The land of my fathers. My fathers can have it – Dylan Thomas

My nan is out of hospital, which is a relief; back where she belongs, in the comfort of her own home. She has a carer come every day, apparently, just for an hour or so, to make sure that she takes her tablets and to clean up a bit. After all, she has had a stroke, just as the nurse said, and her memory is definitely fading a fair bit, but she has always been an independent woman, my nan.

Dad is out in the garden, mowing the lawn. When we got here, he looked out of the window and said hopefully "the lawn could do with a bit of a trim, Joyce." I took a peek myself and it looked like the grass had just had a stern grade two down the barbers, but I knew he was keen to get out in the garden, so I kept quiet.

My nan asks for some help from the kitchen with the two cups of tea she has made, the water boiled in the pan, as usual. Her one arm is still lifeless and limp, but she seems able to make up for it with her other one.

The tea tastes good, with milk and two sugars. I nod my head and smile and listen to my nan excitedly telling me that Mrs Singleton's grandson, is it John or James, oh whatever his name is, anyway, she says, has finally got a job, and back in a confectioners, too. I go to give my congratulations, for it has been almost two years in the job wilderness for Jason now, she has told me often enough, but instead I spit the hot, delicious tea from my mouth. Something isn't quite right. The tea bag is still sitting at the bottom of the cup. I discreetly dip my hand inside and lower the bag into the bin by the side of the settee without being seen.

The house looks pretty good, too. Nan has always been very meticulous, which is probably where my mum gets it from. I'm always fascinated by how similar they are, like two peas in a pod, even though I've never seen them in the same room together, let alone the same pod. She definitely hasn't forgotten where the vacuum and duster is kept, that's for sure. And the place has the same homely feel I always remember. The wedding photo is back in pride of place. I chuckle to myself. It never fails to amaze me how that pretty girl in the photo turned into my sour-faced Aunt Sally.

"So what have you been up to, today, Nan?" I ask, expecting her tell to me, as she usually does, that Mrs Singleton had dropped the newspapers off as she does every morning, that she had completed the crossword, treated herself to a cigarette, watched a bit of TV.

"Today?" she asks, and she looks to the ceiling, as if trying to remember. I wait and wait, until I can't bear waiting any longer, and instead I tell her that this is one of the best teas that she's ever made me.

She smiles at that, and I tell you, my nan has one of the most wonderful smiles in the whole of South Wales. "I do try, Nick," she says. "Don't you go buttering me up, though; I know your game, young man. You'll be expecting lunch now, won't you?" she continues, a cheeky sparkle in her eye. "You've already been eating my *Lockets* as though they were sweets, haven't you?"

My dad is back inside now. There are a few grass clippings sprinkled on his jumper.

"The garden is looking good now, Joyce," he says.

My nan says thank you, dear, but for a moment she looks at my dad as though she is wondering who this strange man is who has just mowed her lawn. My dad does not notice, or maybe he pretends not to notice, and he sits down, picks up a newspaper and starts reading it.

"Still working, Nick?" Nan asks.

Her half full cup of tea dangles precariously from the tip of her middle finger.

"Yes, still at the same place, doing alright, thank you," I say.

"What hours do you work?"

"Just normal office hours, mainly," I reply.

"Nine to five," she chuckles. "Just like Dolly Parton, God rest her soul."

"What about you?" she asks, turning to my dad.

My dad retired years ago and my nan knows this. My eyes stare intently at her cup, for I'm sure the tea is going to topple. She doesn't wait for my dad to respond; he is quite slow in doing so, to be honest, and instead she turns to me and starts talking again, faster, more fluently now.

"Your mother didn't know about dear Albert and her father and it was for the best and I wish I hadn't told her and it would have made everything better," she says, as I reach forward and the tea tips over, staining the carpet.

The three of us busy ourselves, dabbing the tea with kitchen roll, and my nan laughs and comments how silly she had been, all clumsy like that, and my dad seems quite flustered, too. My nan starts telling my dad what a wonderful man he is, that we mustn't take any notice of her babbling away like that, how lucky I am to have him for a father, that he always mows her lawn and looks after her.

I head off upstairs to the toilet, passing Trevor the cat, stretched out on the floor and looking slightly less the lord of the manor than usual. It is as though he has noticed a change in his best friend, and he isn't too sure if he likes it, either. I stare absently through the stained glass window in the bathroom. It has started to rain outside; I can hear it.

I don't really know where I stand with Nan any more, and it's frustrating. One minute she is just like her old self, chatting away and making perfect sense, and I wonder what all the fuss is about. The next she is confused, and her words come out all muddled, like they are in the wrong order or she is using the wrong words or something. But just then, when she spoke about Granddad Albert, she seemed to make no sense at all, and that's the first time I've known that. I wonder whether it's going to become more and more common.

When I go back downstairs, my dad is already on his feet, ready to go. He has already had a goodbye kiss, because the lipstick is smeared on his cheek. My man goes to her handbag and gives me a pound coin for being good.

“Give your mum my love,” she says, as she always does. Then she grips my hand tighter, really squeezes it, until I flinch. “Promise me that you will give your mum my love, dear?”

I promise.

Chapter Twenty One

To create man was a quaint and original idea, but to add sheep was tautology – Mark Twain

"Well, really," my mum says, sinking her petite frame within the depths of the sofa, "I've never, ever been so ashamed in my whole Goddamn life, and that really is saying something, let me tell you."

She lowers her head into the palms of her hands. I look at my dad. He looks at me. Guilt is etched all over his normally placid, expressionless face. This isn't good.

My mum hasn't yet said why it is that she is has never, ever been so ashamed in her whole life, but we both know why, me and my dad, that is. It's down to us, of course it is. We've been waiting more than a week for this moment, for this breakdown. The only surprise is that it has taken so long to come. I almost – and I repeat, *almost* - thought that we had gotten away with it. No such luck.

"Of course," my mum says, managing to prise her hands away from her reddening face, "it would have to have been Hilary Davies that broke the news, wouldn't it? Hilary Davies just couldn't wait to tell me that my own husband – no, it couldn't be somebody else's, could it - that my *only* husband and my *only* son were the talk of the village, the village that I have to live in, every day? And it's not good talk, is it? No; not good talk when it comes to me and my family, of course not."

Dad shuffles and readjusts and then shuffles and readjusts some more.

"I knew as soon as I saw her that she had something she really wanted to tell me," my mum continues. "I was in my own garden, minding my own business, just trimming my own bush, when she rides past on that bike of hers looking like Lady Muck, a big smile on her round ghastly face, greeting me like we were the best of friends. And God only knows that she knows I've never forgiven her for that planning application she put in for that monstrosity of an extension on her house, which everybody but Hilary Davies knows does not fit in with the rest of the village. I knew straight away that something was wrong, right there and then, because she's never usually so nice to me. I ask you, can a lady not be in her own garden, minding her own business, trimming her own bush, without world war three breaking out?"

I had a wicked compulsion to make a gag at this point, but I bit my tongue; I'm surprised that I didn't draw blood.

"Anyway, she said that she had been speaking to Mrs Hopgood. You know Mrs Hopgood, Nick? Robert's auntie from school? You know Robert, couple of years younger than you with the club foot? Anyway, Mrs Davies said that Mrs Hopgood had been speaking to Mrs Williams, and Mrs Williams said that she had caught up with both of you in Monkton fields last Saturday morning…"

And that was it, right there.

I glance at my dad. We are in this together, which I guess makes a change. His eyes fall to the floor. There's suddenly something incredibly interesting on the carpet, like a fluff ball or something. It's all over for us. Hilary Davies isn't an important part of the story. She's merely the messenger, and they say that you shouldn't shoot the messenger, although admittedly, I feel like doing that right now. And Mrs Hopgood – whoever *she* is – is merely a transporter of information. No, the only important person that my mum has spoken about so far is Mrs Williams, and unfortunately Mrs Williams is fundamentally crucial to absolutely everything.

It happened, as my mum quite correctly (as always) said, last Saturday morning. It was a bitterly cold day (even for Bridgend), but despite this, my dad suggested we go for a walk. A walk? Where to? What for? *Just a walk,* my dad said. This was extremely unusual. I was bored in the house though, and so I said yeah, let's go for it.

We crossed the fields behind the house and the grass was marshy and my feet got soaked and I quickly wished that I'd brought some trainers instead of my black leather shoes. We didn't say much, just casual comments about it being cold, and my dad asked if I'd had any more thoughts about the anniversary present, but the relative silence was fine, and to be honest, it was quite nice getting outside in the countryside, enjoying the views, watching the sea rippling in the Bristol Channel.

But it all really happened when we spotted a sheep with his/her head (I just assumed it was a male) trapped in a fence that separated the fields. It was just a normal white sheep (not even a black one) with one of those mysterious blue stripes painted down the width of his body. You could tell that he had been there for quite some time because there was a perfect pyramid of sheep muck at his feet, and that he was pretty distressed about it all. He was doing this constant baahing thing, and not in a happy baahing sort of way, either. We tentatively tried to pull him out, but his head was proper stuck, and we couldn't tear the fence open because there was a thorny hedge in the way.

We were on a proper mission now. There was an unspoken father/son bond between us, and it felt pretty good. We were going to save this sheep and go home as heroes if it was the last thing we did.

My dad had an idea. I'd never seen him so excited. He said that he'd have better access from the other side of the hedge, and so he climbed over the stile and quickly started tearing at the metal wiring of the fence. It would only separate a little though, and so he then started pushing the sheep from the front. I, following suit, started pulling the sheep from behind. The sheep was baahing like mad now, and I shouted excited words of encouragement like, "go on dad, pull him off from the front; I'm pushing real hard from behind."

It was then that I looked over my shoulder and saw Mrs Williams, walking her dog, maybe six metres or so behind me. I smiled at her warmly, my hands gripped firmly either side of the sheep's arse, and to be fair, she smiled warmly back at me. It was then that she saw the sheep, and then my Dad, on the other side of the fence. She stopped dead and so, it felt, did time. There were a few long, terrifying moments before she turned on her heels and walked off in the other direction. At the exact time, in fact, that the sheep pulled free from my loosening grasp and ran off after her, the sound of my dad shouting, "I've just got the big fucker out!" trailing behind him.

My mum is recounting now what Mrs Williams told Mrs Hopgood and what Mrs Hopgood told Hilary Davies and what Hilary Davies told my mum, and it is my turn for my head to be in my hands.

"I just can't believe it," my mum finally concludes, "my only husband and only child are sexual deviants, and Hilary Davies knows all about it."

There is silence in the room. I don't know what to say. It is difficult to choose appropriate words. I start laughing instead, and before I know it, I'm laughing uncontrollably, covering my mouth with my hand. And I'm laughing even more when my dad finally gets to his feet and says "cup of tea, dear?"

Chapter Twenty Two

We are dying from over-thinking. We are slowly killing ourselves from thinking about everything. Think. Think. Think. You can never trust the human mind anyway. It's a death trap – Anthony Hopkins

I look at my watch and observe that it's been three hours since the call. Three hours. I contemplate that it's been one of the longest, most dire three hours of my life.

I'd returned home from work and Mum was in a strange mood, again; stranger than usual, even. She was happy enough, but then there is really nothing unusual about that with my mum. Okay, she moans as much as the next person, but she is an enthusiastic moaner; she makes whatever she is moaning about sound exciting and interesting. *They are campaigning to build another hundred houses right in the middle of the village, Nick,* she would tell me. R*ight in the middle of the village! How absolutely dreadful would that be, I ask you? It would completely obliterate our wonderful view of the sea, and who knows what sort of people it would bring to the village? Mind you, Nick,* she'd say, thumbing her chin and thinking about it for a moment, *it might bring a few more people to the Tuesday night yoga class in the village hall. It has been getting quiet recently, not sure how long it can continue for without more people. So that's a positive, don't you think, Nick?*

There is no doubt that my mum is a livewire, but tonight it was like she'd spent the morning sniffing glue in the downstairs toilet, or something.

"How was work, darling?" she asked, as I came through the front door, planting a kiss on my cheek. "I'm so glad that you are working, Nick," she continued, as I slipped off my shoes (shoes are strictly forbidden on the daily-vacuumed carpet in the Evans household). "There does not seem to be any slack at all with unemployment at the moment, darling. The experts say that it is a double-dip recession. A double-dip recession, of all things! You stick with it. A job is a job, Nick."

I sat down in the kitchen at the round pine table and she brought me a cup of tea, from the pot, of course, none of this tea bag in a mug nonsense (she would go all faint at the mere thought of it), without me needing to ask, and I thought, somebody has changed their tune, haven't they? I took a sip. It was just right. She makes a good cup of tea, my mum, especially considering my dad is the unofficial tea maker. The most me and my mum usually contribute is putting the kettle on. *Who wants a cup of tea?* we'd enthusiastically ask. *I've put the kettle on.* Then we'd look at my dad and he would shrug his shoulders and, without uttering a single word, just go and finish the job off. It's a family tradition.

My mum sat opposite me, arms folded round her chest, leaning forward slightly in her chair, giving me her full attention. She wanted to talk. There was no getting away from it.

"So," she started, "how was it?"

"'It'?"

This 'it' sounded deadly important. I re-traced my day. Got up. Went to work. Came home. There was nothing there worthy of this mighty 'it'. I started worrying now. Had I forgotten something that I should have done today? It wouldn't be the first time.

"Work," my mum said, leaning forward even more.

"Oh," I said, slightly relieved. "Work was just work, I guess. Actually," I continued, remembering something from the day, "my boss took me in one of the little rooms today and said that she was really impressed with the way I had improved my performance."

"Ooh," my mum glowed, "you are doing well! Is there any chance of progression where you are now?"

It wasn't long ago that the idea of me staying there a day longer than I needed to brought her out in one of those womanly hot flushes.

"Not unless the boss dies," I replied, honestly.

"Well, there is always hope, then Nick," she replied, and I

wasn't exactly sure how to take this. "Did I tell you about Jason Thomas, the one who is a distant relative of Mrs Thomas, you know, she lives three doors down from the shop and sometimes rides her bike down to the beach? Anyway, he lives in Aberkenfig, or should I say, he *did* live in Aberkenfig. He got run over by a tractor early morning a couple of weeks ago when he'd fallen asleep in the middle of the road after a night drinking. Didn't stand a chance, did he, the poor thing? Anyway, Nick, I'm just saying, don't give up hope, hey? People can die in the most unexpected of ways, you know."

I wasn't even sure whether this story was true. I hadn't heard of a Jason Thomas getting run over by a tractor, and the local paper usually reports when a kid from the village gets another Cub Scout badge. But then was it really possible that my mum had made up the whole thing to give me hope that there might be an opening in work because my boss could actually die at any moment? I didn't know what to think any more when it came to my mum.

"And how was your day, Mum?" I reluctantly asked.

And it was just how I had expected. She told me everything. How she was almost late for Pilates because she couldn't quite remember whether she had turned the heated brush off, and of course she had to go back and check because it wasn't worth burning the house down, was it, and anyway, the brush was turned off, but that's not the point is it, but she did just make it on time, and there was a new lady there, only just moved into the village and ever so quiet she was but with a lovely smile. And the instructor worked them all harder than usual, all of the girls said so, he must have been in a mood, maybe he had split up with his boyfriend or something? But all the girls felt good afterwards, so it worked out well in the end. Mrs Jones had lost eight pounds since she started coming to the class and it had only been three weeks, that's not bad, is it? Anyway, she didn't go to the pub afterwards, because there were much more important things to be done at home, and she had been polishing the kitchen cabinets when I came home, time just passed so quickly.

There was no doubt about it. My mum had been keeping busy. If she attended enough classes, checked the heated brush and polished enough cabinets, talked and listened at a maddening pace, then maybe there would not physically be enough time to think.

I left her to vacuum the whole house while I lay on the bed, my hands behind my head (something I seem to have picked up from my dad) and just stared into space.

And that's when the phone rang.

"Nick?"

The voice sounded faintly familiar, but only just. It was loud and urgent and hurried.

"Yes," I replied. I wasn't going to ask who it was, but that's what I wanted to ask.

"It's Jan Thornton, Sam's mum."

I sat up now. Anything to do with Sam got my interest.

"Oh, hello, Mrs Thornton," I said awkwardly. Even though she was sweet and lovely and all the things you would ever want in a person, there was still that element of awkwardness, partly because she was my friend's mum, but mainly because that friend had been missing for so many years.

"They have found a body, Nick, and they want me to identify it. Could you come with me, please, Nick?"

And this is where I am now, three hours later. I sit alone now, but it's only been like that for the last six minutes and seven seconds; no six minutes eight, nine, ten seconds. If the last three hours have possibly, probably been the longest hours of my life, then the last six minutes have undisputedly, undoubtedly been the longest minutes of my life. The hours had been spent with Jan Thornton. The minutes had been spent on my own, in complete isolation, with no comfort or support. Now I needed something, anything, like my mother, to stop me from thinking.

She was already waiting in the hospital reception when I arrived. I saw her through the automatic doors, periodically opening and closing, and she was pacing on the hard polished floor, up and down, back and forth. I so wanted to turn round and walk in the opposite direction, just like I had when I saw her what felt like the first time but really it was just the last time, at the leisure centre. It crossed my mind why she had asked me, me of all the people, to come with her, or course it had, but thank God up to that point there had not been much time to think. There had just been a frantic call and then an even more frantic call to the hospital and now here I was. I just figured that she wanted somebody who was not too close to her, who she felt comfortable with. And just like at the leisure centre, I kept on walking forwards.

"Nick," she said, giving me a quick hug. "Thank you so much."

She wore less make-up than the last time I saw her, her face just looked barer and more exposed and less perfect, but conversely, to me, it just made her even more unbearably attractive. There was less mask; less camouflage. She was more real, more like she was when me and Sam were just kids, and she had nothing to prove to anybody. She was undoubtedly terrified, though. Her big blue eyes looked bigger than ever and everything about her seemed fast and precise.

I followed behind her down the corridor. She knew exactly where she needed to go. Bottom floor. Left then right then left. To the section that nobody wants to go to. It felt cold down here. Everything felt clinical. And so clean. Everything looked polished and scrubbed and smelt of disinfectant, even more so than when I had visited my nan. Then there had been the smell of boiled food and people and plastic cups of coffee and tea too, but now that seemed to be taken away and the smell was all the more distinctive and apparent. We sat down on the surprisingly comfortable seats and she held my hand. Her skin felt icy cold, like it had just come out of a freezer.

I knew that every single one of my words needed to be carefully calculated and carefully delivered. Right now a simple, innocent question like *are you alright* seemed like the most stupid, thoughtless three words in the whole dictionary because, of course she was not alright, she was far from alright. *Is there anything I can do to help*, maybe? And yet, what *was* there I could do to help? And so, I just sat there, holding her hand, and it felt just about right.

My mind kept thinking back to when we were kids. It wasn't all that long ago, really, not in the big scheme of things. I'm sure people in their mid forties don't look back on their mid thirties and think wow, that was like a lifetime ago.

There was this time when we were say fourteen and Mrs Thornton dropped me, Sam and Den down at the Merthyr Mawr sand dunes. It was the summer and yet it wasn't the best of days. There was no rain or anything, but it was quite cold and drab. It was a weekday, and the expansive uneven sloping car park full of tree trunks and tiny grey stones was almost empty of cars. I remember how quiet it was, how all that could be heard was the water flowing in the stream and the birds singing and tweeting in the overhanging trees all around; trees that put almost everything on the ground in the shade. Den sat down on a relatively flat and smooth rock by the stream and lit up. He had no intention of doing much, and he could have been anywhere. Sam, on the other hand, was much more energetic, so much more lively and enthusiastic. He crossed the tiny bridge with the wide wooden planks and over the stream, hurriedly tip-toed along one of the narrow footpaths, avoiding the nettles, and I followed behind him, struggling to keep up. The dunes expanded gloriously out in front of us, soft warm yellow sand with dots of grass in little huddles. You knew that the coast wasn't far away, and if you listened really carefully, you could hear the waves crashing against the shore, and yet it felt like a world away. The sandy slopes continued so high that it was impossible to look behind them.

"I freaking love this place," Sam enthused. "There is just so much freedom. You can just be who you like here, at one with nature, and there is nobody to judge you."

He still had glasses then, but gone were the crooked black ones that made him look like a geek. Now he had these designer blue ones that just made him look even cleverer than he was. The lenses were almost impossibly thin and his green eyes were now visible underneath. There was something about the complexity of those beautiful eyes that, more and more as the years passed, drew people in. Sam was growing tall and even though he was still slight (and he remained slight) he just became elegant and distinctive, rather than lanky and awkward, like some of the other boys in our class. I'd overheard a few girls calling Den hunky (but, of course, I never told him) but Sam was more than that. It hurt me to say it at the time, but my best friend was downright pretty.

He left me in his wake that day, exploring one of the paths. I could almost sense him in the distance, enthusing about the different coloured flowers, all the purples and the blues, and the wildlife and nature undoubtedly all around us, if you only knew where to look and what to look for. With my one friend way ahead and my other friend way behind, I decided to settle down on a flat stretch of sand, and allow the time to pass by, slowly and peacefully and quietly.

I was only woken from my daze by a stray grey horse galloping past me, a wild abandoned look in his eyes, and a dripping wet nose. The horse kicked his two front hoofs forward as he saw me. There were plenty of horses down here, they walked along the coastline from Porthcawl to Ogmore, but they were never left to roam alone. This horse had a saddle on, but no rider, and he seemed agitated. There was something wrong. I got to my feet and started running in the direction that he had come.

I had never been very fit, even in those days, and my mouth quickly felt as dry as sandpaper and my legs as heavy as lead, but I kept going. It felt like there was no choice. My feet kept sinking into the uneven ground and then disappearing into hidden divots. I stumbled and fell; my face hit the floor. I spat the sand out of my mouth and for the first time thought about giving up and just walking back dejectedly to the car park, where Den would undoubtedly be comatose waiting for us. But as I looked up, in the distance, I saw Sam.

I got to my feet and ran the final few hundred yards. He was huddled over, one knee on the floor. A girl lay on the sand next to him. She must have only been eighteen or so, but she was still older than us. Her eyes were open but they were glazed, like she wasn't really seeing anything out of them. Sam was holding her hand and she was holding his back.

"She fell off the horse, took a nasty hit to the head. Could you call an ambulance? I haven't got my mobile."

Sam never had his mobile with him. He said he didn't always want to be contacted. And today was definitely one of those days. He was so caring and kind as we waited for the ambulance. He whispered soothing words to the woman, who was called Emma, told her that everything would be just fine, and I for one believed him. He reminded me of a little boy nurturing and caring for an injured bird.

When the medics came looking red faced and out of breath, and they put the girl on a stretcher, we could tell that she was going to be okay. As she was being lifted away, she looked at Sam and mouthed only two words. "Thank you."

Now though, only just over ten years later, his mother has been taken inside a locked room, with a young morbid man in the standard blue uniform, to confirm what we have probably all secretly known, that this kind, caring, beautiful young man is no longer alive.

The key turns and the door unlocks. I get to my feet. Mrs Thornton comes out of the room, her cheeks red and blotchy and her eyes puffy and streaming with tears, and looks straight at me.

It is a look I will never forget for the rest of my life.

Chapter Twenty Three

Sometimes you lose sight of what's going on around you – Usain Bolt

There was nowhere enough room, and only select friends and family had made it inside the church. The rest of the mourners paid their respects in the coldness of the surrounding grounds; the voices of the congregation merely faint echoes seeping through the thick crumbling bricks of the church. Heads were bowed, hands were clasped, tears were wiped, mascara was smeared.

The death made the papers. It was big news. It was not natural for a life so young to be lost; everyone said so. A parent should never, ever have to bury their own child, they continued.

I stand with my back against the black, rusting gates at the entrance to the church grounds. The service concluded. The coffin has been lowered into the ground. I tap my polished shoes on the uneven surface of the path running all the way to the sturdy wooden door of the church. I'm not sure where to look or how to look. I take solace that there are plenty of others here just like me, who look just like me, and an Eminem song starts playing in my head.

It is not a bad day really, I think, trying to distract my mind. Okay, it's cold, for sure, and there is definitely a biting breeze, but the clouds have cleared and the sun has made a rare, welcome appearance.

Jan Thornton walks towards me, her eyes staring intently at the concrete that lies below her clicking heels. She seems smaller than usual; more fragile, almost elf-like. I feel conflicting anxiety with welcome familiarity.

"So very, very sad," she solemnly says, and I nod my head.

I repeat the sentence that I've already heard a dozen or so times this morning: it is good to see you; it's just a shame that it had to be in these circumstances.

I know what she is thinking, and I know she feels guilty just for thinking it. Jan Thornton knows all too well that this could have been her today, that she could have been playing the role of the mother burying her own child, rather than just the bit part she does play. She's only here today to pay her respects to a grieving family who have lost their son.

That look at the morgue has been replaying on my mind every hour of the day.

At first I thought it was the look of a mother who has finally been given the damning verdict, after years of searching and heartache, that her son is dead. Then it dawned on me it was just the realisation the searching and heartache would continue, that it was not, after all, finally over...

Den stands with his hand clasped behind his back, just feet from where his older brother has been lowered into the ground. He looks isolated and lonely. This is not how it should be. I move forward, to be with him, but then I stop. Den turns, and comes face to face with his parents, who are walking painfully slowly back towards the coffin. His father has his arm wrapped tightly and comfortingly around the shoulder of his mother. All three stop walking now, and a confused, awkward look passes between Den and his parents. Den goes to say something, I can see his lips moving and then stuttering and trembling. Either he changes his mind or he cannot think of anything appropriate to say, not in these circumstances, and instead he continues walking, around and past them.

Patrick was killed twelve days ago. There will be countless inquiries and hearings and court cases to endure for the family, but what has never been in dispute is that Patrick Jay Jones was murdered. There was a dispute – a confrontation - and he was stabbed, and from a single wound he bled to death, aged just twenty-seven.

The life that Patrick lived in the eyes of his parents was a lie.

Patrick did have a job, that part was true. It was a basic admin job that probably didn't test him too much, but it did require him to put on a suit and leave the house early every morning. In fact, by all accounts, it all started innocently enough. In the end, though, the job managed to act as a perfect cover for everything else that was going on with Patrick.

He had been on steroids for ages, Den had said as much to me. Patrick had always been a strong boy. In school Den was tall and lean, but Patrick was shorter and stockier, with these thick, mean looking forearms that he liked to display by rolling up his sleeves at every available opportunity. He'd pumped iron and taken drugs, and Den said that he had become, in his own words, a 'massive fucker.' Den said that Patrick became frustrated with everyday steroids – everyone was on them and they didn't give him the edge any more – and he'd started importing from Europe. He got bigger and so did his reputation, and other bodybuilders wanted what he had, and so Patrick bought in bulk and made a tidy profit on the side selling to his muscle-head mates in the gym. Soon he was known as one of the people to go to if you wanted to get sorted. Only, Den said, Patrick never knew when to stop. He got greedy and started dabbling in other drugs, too. It was easy enough to do. He was well known in town. He was able to do deals during his lunch hour and after work, all dressed in his flash designer suit.

The rumours had been flying around about exactly what happened on the night he was murdered, but he was dealing with some pretty shady characters and, by all accounts, they were saying nothing. He was found bleeding to death down a quiet alley just off the main street to the town centre by an old woman who was just taking her dog for a walk. As far as the police were concerned, Patrick was probably just another drugs dealer who had been taken off the streets.

I hadn't seen Patrick since I'd been back in Bridgend, but I knew he'd changed; I just didn't know how much. Den would give me little snippets of information, but it's clear now that he was keeping a lot behind. He said that the guys from football didn't want to play with him because he had a temper. Thinking about it now, they probably didn't want to play with him because he was known as a complete psycho.

The reception is in the family home. All of the downstairs rooms are packed with people of all ages. It is a large, detached house on a private estate. To me, it has always had a peculiarly old-fashioned feel, with wallpaper in every room and thick carpets and wooden ornaments on the fireplace and black and white family portraits on the walls. I've been in the house when it has been just me and Den, and now it feels strange that, in a time of death, it is bubbling with so much life.

Den is dutifully circles the living room. He hands out food on trays, shakes hands politely and thanks people for coming. He is composed and respectful and dignified. I notice that he looks slimmer than last time I saw him. His grey suit hangs a bit on his normally bulky frame. It is no secret that he was familiar with the performance drugs that his brother was selling. He seems to cover every inch of the room and yet somehow, he manages to keep a safe distance from his parents.

His nan has flown over from Jamaica. Den pays her the ultimate respect and attention. She is a shorter, even curvier version of her daughter. I have never met her before but I have always had a picture of her in my mind. She's always seemed a bit legendary. Den has often talked about his nan back in Jamaica, and I've always imagined her sitting on a throne wearing a crown. I have to admit, though, she doesn't seem all that scary to me. I was introduced to her when we got back to the house, and she shook my hand and smiled and thanked me so very much for attending and was concerned that I didn't have any food. It was clear where Mrs Jones got her warmth and elegance from. It's in the genes.

I'm sort of listening to the people in front of me, the ones who are telling me again how sad it all is, how Patrick was such a nice boy, that they are such a nice family and hasn't Den done them all proud today, but really I'm looking over their padded shoulders, keeping my eye on Den. He looks tired and drained. I am worried about him. I have been for some time, if truth be told, but I've done nothing about it. I have been too busy with my own life.

It is getting late and the guests have been trickling out of the door for some time. There are only dribs and drabs remaining. Den has done his bit, really. He catches my eye and nods to the front door.

It's dark outside and colder than I remember it. Den pulls off his tie, which has been lopsided for some time, and pushes it into the top pocket of his suit jacket. It is a quiet estate and he nods or says hello to everybody who passes. We are walking at quite a pace, and at one point I have to jog to keep up with him. We say nothing.

It is warm inside the pub. The barmaid, a lady in her forties, politely says how sorry she is to hear about his brother. The guy on the stool at the bar pays his respects, too. I eye a corner seat with a round table, but Den pushes open the door to the beer garden with his foot and I think of protesting, saying that it is warm in here and cold out there, but I stop and tell myself that it would be total madness to protest about anything at all today.

It is a long narrow garden with wooden benches and a high hedge that keeps even the tallest of men from looking in from the quiet road that runs alongside. The only light comes through the window of the pub, where I can see the outline of the man at the bar, and the orange from the street lights.

Den sits opposite me. A couple of the nails on the bench are loose and I'm slanting. The beer is too cold, but I need it. Den is not talking and I am nervous and there is nothing else to do and so the glass is quickly drained. Den is drinking even faster. I go to the bar and savour the warmth for a few precious moments before returning back outside.

"They know that I knew," Den says, when I sit down.

I have to choose my words carefully. "Knew what, Den?"

He takes a long, full gulp of his pint. "My parents know I knew what Patrick was up to. And they blame me for not saying anything. They haven't said anything, but I can just tell, you know."

So that was what that look was about, I think. It had been playing on my mind since we were at the church, which seems ages ago now. I am just not sure that he is right. That wasn't how I read the look.

I've learnt to be pretty good with words from my jobs, convincing clients and customers to buy this and that, but now I realise that what I've really done is learnt to talk bollocks. What Den needs know are real, genuine words. And I find that I don't know what to say.

"You would have had reasons for not saying anything, Den," I eventually say.

He raises his glass to his mouth. "You know why I didn't say anything? They already had one son they were disappointed in and they at least had one they could be proud of. I just couldn't mess that up for them. The artificial happiness seemed preferable to the grim reality, dude. And besides, I hoped and prayed that Patrick would sort himself out anyway and it would be all okay. And now, mate, I am at his funeral."

This makes sense. It's blatantly true that Den is a big disappointment to his parents. The bit that I haven't been able to work out is why for so long he hasn't even bothered trying to make them proud. In school he always did, right up to the point that he failed his A-Levels. And he did when he was working at the bank, but after that he just seemed to give up, and gradually morphed into what he is now.

I remember the first time he came to visit me in University. It was in November, a couple of months after I'd started and Sam had gone missing. He caught the train up to Hull on a Friday night and was still in his suit. There was me in my tatty clothes, living mainly off a diet of frozen burgers and baked beans, and here was my old mate, looking dapper and mature. It was difficult to imagine that we were the same age. He excitedly talked about what he had been up to in the office. He said that he liked to stay late and get stuff done after everyone had left and it was just him and the cleaners. He was earning money, though it wasn't much, but I was living on nothing, and I was proper envious of my mate.

But it didn't last. Den visited me in the third year, when I was close to finishing and I already had a job set up in London, and the transformation was incredible. He came up on a Friday night again, but this time he wasn't in a suit but in jeans that had holes all over them, and he was pissed by the time I met him at the station. He said that he had been sacked, but he didn't give a proper reason; he just mumbled something about there being a disagreement. All weekend he was hard on it, smoking and drinking and pulling birds. It was as if I'd grow two years older and he had grown two years younger.

"You know what?" Den asks now. "Mum phones Nan in Jamaica every Sunday, and tells her everything about anything." It reminded me of my calls from London to my mum. "Nan always used to ask how I was getting along first, because I was the son with the most potential, you know?" He stabs his chest with his finger. "But Nan never asked any more. Mum told her how Patrick was doing in his job, instead. Nan knew that he was doing well, because he was sending money back to Jamaica, just like I used to. That's when they know you're doing well. What's the point in coming over here unless you're going to learn and earn money? Dad had done well, because he had studied and got a qualified job and bought a house. And now Patrick, they all thought, was going to do the same."

He is slurring his words a bit, which surprises me because we are only on our second pint, and Den can handle his drink. He must have been drinking back at the house, I think. Either that or the emotion of it all is hitting him.

I think again about Patrick when he was working. I guess he must have made not only his parents proud, but all his family back in Jamaica, including Nan, proud, too.

"I haven't slept a wink, I've been so worried about it all," Den continues.

"You didn't sleep at all last night?" I query, worried.

Den thinks about this. "You what?" he asks, confused. "It's just an expression isn't it? I mean, I slept okay, really. You telling me that when people say they haven't slept a wink, they actually mean they really haven't slept a wink, yeah?"

I nod my head, a bit baffled, and I'm not sure whether he will be able to see my outline in the darkness.

"That really is some crazy shit," Den says.

I think it is time to change the subject.

"We never did work out the true definition of 'banter?" I meekly offer, not that it seems to matter now.

But Den seems to pick up a bit at this. I can sense him sitting up. "I've thought about it a fair bit; I guess it's been to distract my mind a bit, you know? I think we have our definition of the word, but anyone else can have their own, its up to them."

"But do you think that lady was right with her definition?" I ask.

"Do I fuck!" Den says, and I can see him waving his hand, dismissively, and I laugh at this.

"Why did you get sacked from the bank all those years ago, Den?" I ask.

"It was to do with Patrick," he mumbles, and finishes his drink. He jumps to his feet and goes to the bar without even asking if I want another, and returns with two pints.

"He would come into the branch and visit me with his mates," he continues, as though he hadn't just left mid-conversation. "He wasn't exactly doing much at the time and, to be honest, Pat coming there didn't make a great impression. The boss's wife worked at the bank, too, and she was a bit of a looker, all legs and big tits, like. She gave the impression that she was game, too. At first Pat came to visit me, but then I just became an excuse to chat this woman up, like. The boss obviously didn't like him sniffing around his wife, and things changed for me. The boss made things difficult and wanted me out. The guy got it into his head that Patrick had shagged his wife, you know, and there was no going back from there. Some money went missing and he blamed me. I think it was a set-up, if I'm honest with you. It didn't matter, though. I was out."

I try to absorb this information. So he lost his job because his boss thought Patrick was shagging his wife?

"So did Patrick actually do anything with her?" I ask.

Den laughs now, and it is the deep throaty laugh I know and love. I realise it's the first time I've heard him laugh all day.

"Pat said that she couldn't get enough of his length."

I laugh too, even though, in these circumstances, it really shouldn't be funny. I guess it might be because this is the Patrick that we both remember, all those years ago.

"So why did you go off the rails so much, then, Den?" I ask.

I've never felt so brave, or stupid, or inappropriate. I don't know whether I have just given up searching for the right words, but somehow this feels about right. I hear kids playing on the road beyond the hedge, and a tennis ball plops on the grass next to our bench. It's a hairy thing with a chunk missing from the side, like it has been chewed by a dog or something. I can't help but glance at it out the corner of my eye. Den, though, doesn't even appear to have noticed.

"I'll be honest with you, mate; I pretty much just thought fuck it. I studied like a madman to pass my exams in school. I was up all night on caffeine drinks and by the time I took them I was as high as a kite, know what I mean? And I worked my little Jamaican ass off at that bank job and look where it got me? When I lost my job, you should have seen the look my dad gave me. The thing was, they expected a lot from me, you know. Patrick was the letdown. I was the potential. And right then I thought, fuck this, I'm never going to give them these crazy high hopes again. Now I've been a disappointment so long they just expect it. It's been so much easier, dude."

I remember somebody saying that they were a perfectionist; if they can't do something perfectly they just don't bother doing it at all, and it seems real canny right now.

"Did you tell your parents that Patrick lost you that job?"

Den shakes his head.

"Sounds like he owed you one," I say.

"I guess," he accepts.

"And how do you feel about all of it now, then?"

He pauses before answering. My friend has been in full flow, not even pausing for breath.

"You know, it feels like I'm the hope again. My parents haven't got Pat to rely on any more. It is all on me again now. Only, this time, like, it's like I'm all they've got, so I can't fuck it up this time. And I don't think I'm up to it no more, to be honest," he says.

It is my turn to think. "I think that now they only have one son, you'd be surprised what would make them happy, Den," I say.

For the first time in what feels like ages, we sit in silence, just like we did when we first came outside. It feels colder than ever. The breeze sweeps through the garden, and my empty pint glass rattles on the sloping wooden bench.

"You know your dreams, about Sam? I get them, too, you know."

This hits me hard. Den has never mentioned this before. I thought it was just me.

"Yeah, but they are a bit different. We don't meet up when we are younger, in school uniforms or any of that strange stuff. We are mates now and we just have a laugh. The thing is, though, I always know that it is a dream, and he always knows that he isn't really a part of our lives anymore, and so we make the most of every second because we all know that as soon as I wake up, Sam will no longer be here. I kind of treasure the dreams, you know..."

I don't know what to say.

"So the last time you saw him," I eventually begin, "you know, the day that we picked up our exam results, did he give you any indication that he, you know, wasn't happy, like? You know – like he would do something stupid?"

It had been a tough final year in school, I guess. I always recall that night down the beach because it's the last time I remember everything being just right. We were all going to do our final year in school and then head for Uni. It had always been the plan. That night, things were still in our hands. And yet a year later, I was the only one that actually went.

Den was like a machine when he returned to school for that final year. He was on a mission to get straight As. The kid was always in the library, in his usual seat, studying. He started changing, week by week, before our eyes. He'd always been a bit of a swot (although some kids in school would have replaced the 's' with a 't'), but the guy was still one of the first to crack a joke and a smile. He became much more serious. He worried about his grades. You could see him tensing up. I guess he'd already sunk long before he got to that economics exam hall, really.

Sam definitely changed, too, but with him it was much harder to pinpoint exactly how. Unlike Den, he breezed through his exams; that wasn't a problem. I think it was more of a growing up thing with Sam. He'd become a hit with the ladies, that's for sure. Okay, you could tell that they thought he was beautiful, but it was more than that. The guy actually knew how to talk to them. He seemed to relate to them, whereas to Den and me they were still most definitely from Mars, or is it Venus, or more excitingly, Uranus? We were both totally jealous of our friend. Sam began hanging around with his own group of girl mates just as much as he hung around with us. But he was still such a bubbly, fun guy, it was impossible to feel bitter. The bond was still there. We were still the Three Amigos. That hadn't changed. Looking back, I think I always felt there was something on his mind that he wanted to tell us, but felt he just couldn't.

We picked up our exam results from school in the morning. There was no surprise that Sam had passed with flying colours, and I managed to scrape through with passes, but of course, Den failed them all. The guy was trying to put on a brave face, but it was obvious that he was upset. We were just moping around town together, and it wasn't doing any of us any good. Sam suggested we do something different. We jumped on a bus and ended up in the heart of Garw.

I remember thinking that even though it was less than ten miles or so from the centre of Bridgend, it felt like a different world. There were rows and rows of small, sloping, terraced houses with black smoke piping through the chimneys. One long road stretched all the way through the middle; all the other roads spiralled and twisted but to nowhere in particular, and to me it felt like it was to oblivion.

And yet Sam was in his element. He loved the solitude and the peacefulness. There was no doubt that beauty was all around us, but I don't think I would have taken it in if Sam had not been so enthusiastic. He loved the quietly flowing streams and the forestry that expanded into the mountains.

Sam thought that it was full of secrets and possibilities, places to hide away and explore. The three of us walked to nowhere in particular, but for the first time since we were together on that beach a year earlier, things felt just right.

"No, it was a good day," Den says, his voice a little unsteady. "At the time it felt like it was more about me, because you two were heading to University and I wasn't going anywhere, like? But in the valleys Sam was happier than I ever remember, and I've thought about that day a whole lot, you know, replaying it again and again in my mind? I guess the only thing that really stands out for me is the hug he gave me when I got to my house. It was a happy hug for sure, and fair enough, I wasn't going to see him for a while because he was off to Leeds, like. But I always wondered whether he knew then that he wasn't going to see me again. That he wasn't just saying I'll see you in a few months, but that he actually was saying a final goodbye to me, you know?"

I did know. He had given me the same hug, I remember now. I just hadn't realised the significance before. Or maybe I hadn't wanted to realise the significance. So Sam was planning something. So they had been right, all along.

Den stands up and holds out his hand. It is a straightforward shake this time, without any of the extra moves that he sometimes offers.

"Thanks mate," he says. "I really love you, man."

He turns and walks through the little gap in the hedge.

I sit there, shivering, wondering why the kids didn't come looking for their tennis ball.

Chapter Twenty Four

No leadership, no ideas. Not even enough imagination to thump someone in the line-up when the ref wasn't looking – JPR Williams

I knew that my dad had his eye on watching *DIY SOS*, and truth be known, so did I, and so when my mum dropped her bombshell, it really was a bit of a shocker.

"Why don't we go to the pub for a nice drink together, just the three of us? It would be just me and my two favourite men."

I glanced at Dad and he glanced at me too. A tuft of greying hair stood up on one side of his forehead. There was instantly a united bond, just as there had been when the sheep incident came to light. He didn't want to go to the pub, either.

"There are plenty of drinks in the cabinet," I offered. "I can pour you one of those strawberry Baileys if you like, I know it's your favourite, Mum."

I sprang to my feet before she could raise an objection, but I was too damn slow.

"No, thank you darling, but I'd like to go out for a change. I never seem to go out anywhere."

Now it was my dad's turn to pull something out of the bag. I am sure I glimpsed a solitary bead of sweat trickle down his sloping forehead.

"*DIY SOS* is on a bit later, love," he blurted.

He had cracked, and so here the three of us are, in the pub together on a weekday night.

And it is happy days, if truth be known. The reality is that neither of us would have let Mum down. We both know how much she has been worrying about my nan, although it's not good form for our family to openly talk about it. Now, my mum really is somebody who hasn't been sleeping a wink. She has been looking tired; the dark shadows under her eyes have been becoming more and more a part of her everyday look. But she is trying hard, as she always does. She has taken time to look good tonight, and she certainly does look like a lady who takes care of herself. And she is glowing, even if the smile has been plastered on.

We sit in the corner, watching people trickle in and out through the swinging door. There are only a small handful of people in here, and they are all locals, all regulars. The round wooden table we occupy has more dents in it than a dart board and it threatens to topple over every time we lean against it. The *Brains Bitter* beer mats are soaked through and tearing apart. But it all feels homely, and it's nice to be out with my folks.

Plus, I am safe in the knowledge that I caught my dad sneaking into the lounge and recording *DIY SOS.*

The black Labrador, Jesse, who belongs to the pub, lazily rests his chin on the flat of my feet. My mum tells all the regulars that the dog has a soft spot for me. They nod their heads and think of something witty to say. Most say silent. I wish that she wouldn't go on about it too much, though. There is a big sign above the entrance asking that you refrain from feeding the dog. Last time I was in here, I fed him pork scratchings under the table. I suspect that Jesse has a good memory when it comes to pork scratchings.

A local, Dean Morgan, is sat on his own on a high stool close to the bar. I've already seen him down three pints of Guinness since I've been here. He looks a bit worse for wear, and that really is saying something, since I imagine he has the constitution of a horse.

Dean must stand 6'4" in his boots. He is the kind of guy who walks through doorways sideways. His hands are like shovels and his dark stubbly chin looks pricklier than a cactus.

My mum breathlessly observes that Dean is getting older. I nod my head. Must be in his forties now, I imagine. His two daughters must be ten or so now, I calculate. They are his pride and joy, following him everywhere around the village. Mind you, the guy is a bit of a legend round here. He owns his own building firm, and he is always the first choice for the locals. The kids look up to him; he is their gentle giant of a dad. He does alright for himself, too. I notice that he looks bigger than ever, but that his massive bulk is padded with a layer of fat that wasn't there before. He arches his head back, opens his mouth wide, and downs half a pint in one go; then walks unsteadily to the bar.

"Dean seems to be having a good night tonight," my mum chuckles admiringly.

That is one of those things with my mum. If either I or, God forbid, my dad was sat in the corner of the pub getting drunk on countless pints of Guinness, she would hide with shame. If Dean Morgan does it, it just makes him all the more lovable.

Mind you, I would never say anything derogatory within spitting distance of Dean. He is, as they say in the films, 'not somebody to be trifled with.' I recall this one time I came here with Dean and Sam. We were only eighteen, and it wasn't long before Sam went missing. For a short while it became quite the in thing to come down the coast on Friday nights. Groups of teens would catch the bus down, get drunk, and then, hopefully, catch the last bus back into town. That night, a group of five lads from the year above us in school (they were then in college), got absolutely smashed. They were standing on the old creaking stools playing drinking games and shouting and singing. The three of us sipped our beers and watched with bated breath.

It got late and Keith, the normally affable landlord, had had enough. He asked them to leave, pleasantly enough. He didn't want any hassle, not Keith. One of the boys told him to go fuck himself. All the others started cracking up. Keith couldn't really do anything about it. He busied himself by polishing the bar, pretended that nothing had happened. But it was embarrassing for the guy. This was supposed to be his manor. I felt sorry for him.

Dean was there, as normal, in his usual seat, drinking Guinness from the jar that Keith kept behind the bar for him. He was with his wife that night.

He swivelled in his stool so that he faced the young lads. He reiterated that the landlord had asked them to leave. Dean didn't even raise his voice. He had bigger balls than me, I can tell you. The lads weren't put off, though. There were five of them and the beer had made them big men, I guess. They stumbled around, spilling more drink on the old carpet.

"You can go fuck yourself, too!" one of the boys grinned. I still remember his face now, all red and sweaty.

Dean stood up and walked over to the guy. He was wearing his usual heavy boots and his jeans were stained from a day on the building site. He towered over the kid. Dean laid into him with a single right cross. I winced from behind my pint as the lad fell to the floor. One of the boys charged with his head down, arms flailing like a windmill. Dean took a step to the side and caught the boy with a thump on the back of his head, as the boy tumbled into a table. Glasses smashed and there were a few screams as the table toppled over and onto the floor. Another lad picked up a chair and threatened Dean with it, but he didn't look so brave any more. Dean just shook his head and swiped the chair from him. He threw it against a wall and it smashed into pieces. The boy raised his knees high to his waist to protect himself. He looked like a kid in the playground, whimpering. It was a game of cat and mouse now. The remaining youngsters dodged around Dean and ran out of the door.

I think I mentioned that it was only for a short while that it became the in thing to catch a bus down to the coast on a Friday night.

And that is just one of the stories about Dean Morgan. There are plenty of others.

My mum is at the bar now. She insisted that she get a round in; said something or other about being a modern lady now. She tells Keith that Jesse has a soft spot for me.

"He hasn't been feeding him under the table, has he?" Keith asks.

I decide to engross myself in conversation with Dad, which is easier said than done.

"Dean looks a bit down tonight, Dad," I say.

"He's alright, our Dean. He's a sound enough bloke."

Things had been a bit awkward between the two of us since I'd raised the valuation with him last week. I'd waited for the right time. My mum was on the computer upstairs, engrossed in the online IT course that she had recently enrolled on. There was just me and him in the lounge. I lowered the sound on the TV and nervously told him that I'd done something wrong, that I had gone in his shed and taken two of his paintings to a valuer but I stressed with great enthusiasm that the man said he had real talent, and that he even offered money for the paintings.

The room went silent. My Dad avoided eye contact. I was really worried how he would react. I had been in his shed, after all. It was his sanctuary, his place. He sat up and put his hand on his chin.

"It's good to know that I can paint a bit, son," he finally said. "That really is very nice, and I appreciate you doing all this for me. But I'm just happy how I am, Nick, just spending some time doing my own thing in the shed, like I always have, with no pressure, you know? Could you do me a big favour please and not mention any of this to your mum for me?"

I was a bit frustrated by this. It was a real chance for him to show that he had talent of his own, that he wasn't always in her shadow.

"But you could make her real proud of you, Dad!" I protested.

He looked me in the eyes now, and again spoke softly. "I think she's already proud of me, son, don't you think?"

I guess his reaction didn't upset me, not really. In a way I was relieved that he wasn't angry with me. It just felt like a waste, that's all.

I raise my glass now and clink his. "I promise I won't say anything to Mum about the paintings, okay Dad?" I say. He gives me an appreciative nod.

And that's when it happens.

Mum returns from the bar, carefully balancing three drinks in her hands. Dean says something to her. I cannot make out what he says. His voice is deep and muffled and his words are slurred. My mum heard, though. She looks shocked, horrified even. And Dad heard too.

My dad drags back his chair. I watch, horrified. He stands

up and walks over to Dean. Even on his stool, Dean seems to dwarf his diminutive figure.

He takes a swing at Dean with his right fist. The punch lands square on the chin. There is a connection. The stool wobbles. My mum screams. Keith puts his hands over his eyes. Dad stands with his arms by his side, fists still clenched.

"Don't you ever speak to my wife like that, Dean," he says.

Dean rubs his hand over his chin. He looks more perplexed than anything, like he wonders whether that actually happened. His big dark eyes look hollow. The whole pub goes quiet. There is going to be a tear up. My dad is gong to be hospitalised, or worse.

Dean stands up from his stool. He towers over my dad, who looks like a boy next to him. I wait for the punch. Dean brings back his hand.

And then he offers it to my dad.

"You're right, Charlie," Dean says. His head is lowered. He does not keep eye contact. He is clearly embarrassed. "I am sorry. I think I've had too many drinks tonight. It won't happen again. You got my promise on that one."

The two men shake hands.

Back home, my dad brings me a cup of tea and a couple of biscuits. His forehead looks shinier than ever. He is still my dad, but he seems different now, somehow. We both dip the biscuits into the tea. I remember the joke Den made about dabbing biscuits in Viagra before dipping them, to keep them hard. My mum is a bundle of nervous energy. I hear the vacuum cleaner in one of the other rooms. Nobody mentioned the incident in the pub. I know it is a closed door.

I don't know what Dean said to my mum, and I guess I never will know. It must have been bad, though. I sort of understand a bit more why my dad was the Union representative at the Council.

It is like he said, though. Dean is a sound enough bloke. All I really know, though, is that however much respect my dad has for Dean Morgan, it isn't nearly as much respect as Dean Morgan has for my dad.

Chapter Twenty Five

I love him because he is Welsh and stylish...and because he gave me those shoes – Dame Shirley Bassey

"So do you think Den will be okay then, Nick?" Sara asks.

It is the early hours of Sunday morning and we have just had sex.

Earlier in the week - it was probably Tuesday or Wednesday - Sara placed her customer on hold and started whispering to me. She does not whisper often. She is much more prone to shouting, and so I knew that whatever she wanted to tell me must be important. Sara asked whether I'd like to take her on a proper date this weekend. I said that would be nice. She smiled and said that she was washing her hair this weekend, but it was nice to know that I'd like to take her out, anyway.

It felt dead exciting, going on a proper date. It reminded me of my first ever date, when I was fifteen and a girl called Claire Hewitt asked me out. She was a nice girl, with a loud laugh and a big smile and even bigger boobs. To be honest, she'd asked quite a few of the other boys out by the time she got to me and it sort of felt like it was my turn. My dad dropped me off at Bridgend station and we caught the train to Cardiff together. We went to the cinema and watched *Terminator 3.* I wanted her think that I was a manly sort of man. I kissed Claire in the cinema but it was dark and I bit her lip, and she wasn't happy. On the Monday morning it was all around the class that I'd bitten her. She made me sound like I was Dracula. Her laugh sounded louder than ever that day.

It gave me an idea, though. I just *had* to take Sara to the cinema. That is what a proper date is all about, I thought. Dad dropped me off at Bridgend train station, just like he did ten or so years ago, and I caught the train to Cardiff. Only,

Sara did not catch the train from Bridgend with me; she met me at Cardiff station.

Just catching the train at Bridgend takes me down memory lane, even though I do it now nearly every day for work. It reminds me of when I was fourteen and I caught the train to Swansea with Den and Sam. It was just for a day out; somewhere different from Cardiff and Bridgend. There was a black man waiting on our platform. He was about fifty and had a stocky build. I thought it had to be Glenn Webb, the winger for Bridgend during the eighties, well known as the first black player to be capped for Wales. I told Sam and Den that Glenn Webb was waiting for the train, too. Only, Den, started going mad.

"You telling me you see a black guy in Bridgend and he has to be Glenn Webb, yeah?" he shouted at me, exasperated. "That guy over there must be seventy, plus he's about five foot tall!"

On closer inspection, the guy at the station was older and shorter than I'd initially thought. The funniest part about it, though, was Sam's reaction. He thought it was hilarious. He laughed like a hyena. There were tears in his eyes. And from then on he stirred it for all it was worth. Whenever we were all together and we saw a black guy, he'd go, "is that Glenn Webb?"

He even did it one time when we met Den's dad.

I took Sara to watch *Avengers*. It was a mid-afternoon showing and we had plenty of room. There was no kissing this time and so, thankfully, no biting of her lip. As we rode the escalator afterwards, I asked Sara whether she enjoyed the film. She said yes, that it was full of male crumpet. I was not sure whether or not I felt jealous. When we came out of the cinema, it was still daylight.

"What have you got planned for me next then, Nick?" Sara asked, flirtatiously, brushing her arm against mine.

Oh, I thought that *was* the date. I paused for a moment, frantically trying to think of a second part I could invent.

"What time are Mummy and Daddy expecting you back?"

Sara has this strange notion that I'm a bit of a mummy's boy.

"I roll however and whenever I please," I replied, kind of coolly.

"Let's go to Roath Park, then."

And it was as simple as that. We caught the bus, and because it had not been planned and it was not expected, it felt exciting. I thought; this girl knows how to have a good time.

It was the first time I'd been to Roath Park with a girl. I always loved it when Nan took me there; I ran around everywhere and slid down the highest slides in the playground. I was only seventeen, after all (joke). This time, though, it was different. We held hands as we strolled around the grounds, gazing at the rowing boats in the lake and admiring the array of beautiful flowers. I felt just so incredibly relaxed.

A few hours later and we were in bed together.

It was not planned, but I guess it was hardly a surprise. We had been growing closer and closer over the past few weeks and months and we were becoming increasingly flirtatious. Kissing felt like a natural step after holding hands in the park. Base two and three and so on quickly followed.

And so we lie together in her bed in the early hours of the morning. There's a slight gap in the curtains and only the faintest light snakes through. We are both just outlines and shadows. Sara rests her face on my chest. My arm has slipped around her waist. It feels like we are old, familiar lovers.

I never imagined for a moment that Sara would be the sort to roll over, light up a fag and then start snoring. I suspect that she never sleeps at all.

She is always curious, always interested; forever asking questions and listening to your answers.

I'd been thinking about this question every day since the funeral, and I still had no clue what the correct answer was.

"I hope so," I say, feeling her delicate breaths against my chest. "I knew that things weren't right with Den, but I had no idea he was this – well – this screwed up. He feels more pressure than ever now. He thinks he's the only hope left."

There's a few seconds silence. "Do you think the extra

pressure is a good thing? You said that he has hardly been pushing himself for years, isn't it?" Sara asks.

I think about this for bit. "I think it will be a bad thing if Den lets it be a bad thing, for sure. I think he just needs to look at it from different eyes and he will be okay."

I am not even sure what I am saying myself or whether I have said it right, but Sara just kisses my chin and says that she thinks, "I'm dead right."

And then, totally unexpectedly, her breathing becomes slower, louder, more nasal and she starts (very femininely) snoring. So she does sleep, after all.

I really don't want morning to come.

Chapter Twenty Six

Green door, what's that secret you're keeping? – Shakin Stevens

We had been knocking on the green wooden door for what felt like an eternity when an old man with a flat cap, green wellingtons and a weathered, ruddy face yelled to us from the other side of the street.

"You looking for the old lady who lives at number eight?" he asked, pleasantly enough, to be fair.

I tugged at my father's sleeve; he was that agitated. "Of course we are!" he yelled back from our side of the street.

"It's just," the man continued, undeterred by dad's rant, "when I looked out of the window earlier to check for the postman, because he was late as usual, I saw her walking down the street, wearing one of her dresses, looking ever so smart she was, you know how she takes pride in herself, only she was wearing her slippers, these flat-soled comfortable looking ones, and I thought that I must get myself a pair of those, and I was going to ask where she got them from when she got back, only when I was sitting down watching *Loose Women* with a cup of tea a bit later, I wondered whether it was all a bit strange, you know?"

"Which way did she go?" my Dad demanded, obviously in no mood for any niceties.

"That way," the man pointed.

We followed the hand at a determined pace, unspeaking.

And now, two hours later, my nan is still missing. We decided to split, double our chances, just like they do in the movies, and yet all it's managed to do is halve my hopes and quadruple my emotions. I cannot help but think that Nan could be absolutely anywhere, with anyone, doing anything; my dear, frail, vulnerable Nan. My fingers look pink and raw and feel numb, and I think that if I feel this way, how on earth must she be feeling right now?

My phone, snug and tight in my right trouser pocket, vibrates, and I grab for it. It's Mum. She is the last person I want to speak to right now. No; right now I want to speak to my dad, and with good news. This is only going to panic her. It is *her* mother, after all. But I answer it. What choice do I have, really? *Try to act normal*, I tell myself. She knows something is up, straight away; she always does. She calls me Nicholas and demands to know what is wrong. I tell her that I have a cold, that I've just missed the bus; that I'll be home shortly. She doesn't believe me. And so, I tell her that Nan is missing, and the phone goes dead.

There is no rationality behind my searching. Any direction seems as promising, or as hopeless, as the next, and so I wander down by the pond, probably because it is more appealing than all those dark backstreets. There are a few ducks, just casually swimming around on top of the water as usual, with no complexities, no drama, no crisis. I envy the simplicity of it. I'm sure that they do not worry where their lives are going, and anyway, what is the point of it all, really? And then there are the tattered dirty sleeping bags which are always there, on the path that surrounds the pond, sheltered by the beautiful overhanging trees, thin bony bodies lying somewhere inside the bags, lifeless either because of sleep or drink, or maybe both. I look closer. Right now, anything that even slightly resembles human life in some shape or form has become a suspect.

I blow as much heat as I can muster into my hands and slump down onto a park bench, overlooking the pond with the ducks and the homeless people. My body feels exhausted. I remember the last time I saw my nan, was it two days ago now? It feels like weeks or months. It is hard to forget, though. She was still my wonderful, dear nan, smiling infectiously, her chatter constant and amusing.

My phone vibrates again. This time it *is* my dad.

"Come down to St James church, son, your mother has found her."

I move fast, and this time there is direction in my movements. My despair quickly turns to elation and then to confusion. I'd tried the chapel where my granddad Albert is at rest and where my nan goes to pay her respects every week, without fail, even over the last few, difficult months. My dear granddad Albert, who passed away before I was born, and who everyone said, especially my mum, was one of the kindest gentlemen you could ever wish to meet. *The last of the real gentlemen,* she would tell me, over and over, when I was a kid. But he was buried at the chapel. I could not understand for the life of me why my nan would be found at St James church.

It isn't far, and I am moving fast. Steam from my breath fills the air around my pink cheeks. My loose jeans (all that work at the gym must be paying off) rub against my hips as my feet walk faster than my legs can go.

The church is only around the corner now, and I've no idea what to expect. It's my nan I see first. She is smiling, and I tell you, it is most definitely the best smile in the whole of South Wales. And the kind old man with the flat cap, green wellingtons and a weathered ruddy face was right when he said that she was looking ever so smart, for the blue flowery dress that falls down by her ankles is one of her old favourites. She is embracing my mother, who has her back to me. Mum is holding my nan tight, as if she is scared to let her go. Dad is by their side, awkwardly pacing round and round in a circle.

It feels colder than ever in that graveyard. I give my father a smile, and he gives me a relieved, knowing smile back. Right now, right here, we are relative outsiders. It was my mum who had found her, and that is because she knew Nan the best. It no longer matters that they haven't spoken to each other for all the time that I'd been alive. When it really mattered, and I mean *really* mattered, my mum knew exactly where my nan could be found.

And that's when it hit me. My nan had the heel of one of her slippers (now all muddy and stained) pressed against a gravestone. It was not the gravestone of my granddad Albert, the last of the true gentlemen, for he was resting in the chapel. I thought back to what my Nan had said in her house the last time I'd seen here, when she was all confused and dazed. *Your mother didn't know about dear Albert and her father and it was for the best.* Not all of her words were confused, and she was not completely dazed.

She was referring to two people. Dear Albert. And her father.

But right now, standing in this bitterly cold and drab graveyard with my mum, dad and nan, with many more questions than answers, it really does not matter; not right now. All that really matters is that my Nan is safe and that for the first time in my life, we are all together, as a family.

Chapter Twenty Seven

Once upon a time I was falling in love but now I'm only falling apart. There's nothing I can do, a total eclipse of the heart – Bonnie Tyler

The honeymoon was blissful. Sara put more customers on hold than ever and whispered sweet things to me. Then she put other customers on hold and whispered crude things to me. We had secret liasons in the drinks area. I was Brad and she was Angelina. And what made it more exciting was that it was our little sexy secret; nobody else knew a thing.

The beginning of the end began on Thursday morning. Pam took me into one of the meeting rooms.

"I'm retiring, Nick," she said flatly. "I've kept it quiet, because, you know me, I don't like any fuss, but my last day will be in three weeks."

Wow, I thought, this was big news indeed.

"Funny thing is," I laughed, "I was saying to my mum only recently that the only way you'd ever leave was if you died, and here you are, retiring."

I thought about this for a moment and concluded that it probably wasn't the best thing to say. Pam was laughing, though. I had noticed recently that she seemed a lot more relaxed about things.

"I'm sixty-two now, Nick, and I don't feel I've got the same spark that I once did. I think it's time to just put my feet up and enjoy myself."

"I think you deserve it, Pam," I said, honestly.

"Anyway, I'll get to the point. An advert will be going out internally for my role. We need to give everybody an opportunity to apply. However, I would really like you to go for it, Nick."

Pam continued to tell me, with great enthusiasm, that I'd impressed her greatly over the last few months, and that although I can appear a bit dopey and that some of the staff make fun of me behind my back – which was news to me – they all really respected me and would respond well to me as a leader. She said that they trusted me for calling a spade a spade. Mike would be a contender for the role, for sure, but he had a few barriers, and I would be right up there with him.

There seemed like only one thing to say in response to all this.

"Why can I sometimes appear dopey?" I asked.

The honeymoon was still in full flow at that point.

Next morning, Karen strolled into the office fifteen minutes late and shouted to anybody who would listen, "Sorry I'm late; I was up all night reading that *Fifty Shades of Grey.* I tell you, that Christian Grey, the things I'd let him do to me…"

I remember thinking that team management was probably more stress than it was worth.

The email announcing Pam's imminent retirement and her vacancy went out just before lunch. There was an instant wave of shock and excitement.

Which is really when the beginning of the end became just the end.

"Can you believe that Pam is leaving?" Sara enthused as soon as we were alone together, on our bench just down the road from the office. "I thought that she would be leaving in a coffin!"

I told her that I had been informed about it the day before, and that Pam had expressed an interest in me applying for the vacancy. I'd been a bit reluctant telling Sara, as I thought she might feel bad about me being asked and not her. I really wasn't sure how she would react. She had told me herself that she would never progress because she just couldn't resist being cheeky to the customers.

"Oh my God!" she said. "That's amazing, Nick!" She gave me a kiss on the cheek. "You've done really well! You were really shit when you started, like! I'm sure you'll get the job now. It would be amazing having you as my manager."

There seemed like only one thing to say in response to all this.

"You thought I was shit when I started?" I asked.

Sara just laughed.

"I don't think I'll go for it, though," I said.

She looked really confused.

"Why not?"

"I don't want to be stuck in this place forever," I replied, honestly. "I was only ever supposed to be here as a temporary measure. Cath from the recruitment agency said that it was just to get my feet back on the ground. I have a degree, for God's sake. And I had a really good job in London. I don't want to be here in say three years time wasting my life away."

"Like me, you mean?"

"No, I mean, you haven't got a degree or anything have you? So I guess you have nowhere better to go…oh I don't mean it like that…"

"No, I know *exactly* what you mean, Nick, and you are absolutely right."

Only, if she agreed with me and I was absolutely right, it still did not stop her from getting up off the bench and marching off.

It was becoming more and more clear to me that I took too much notice of my own problems and not enough of those closest to me.

Days passed with Sara just grunting and sighing at me when I passed her in the drinks area or by the lifts. On one, difficult occasion, we were waiting for the same lift and she shut the doors before I could get in. The reason for the argument became a distant memory. The promotion was put to the back of my mind. I passed my working days by taking call after call and working like a zombie. My sales figures were never better.

And so I work the late shift. Sara was on the early, which gives me a few hours where I can feel a little easier. I quite like the late shift. It is quieter and cosier. Half of the lights have been switched off. The darkness outside means I can stare at my own reflection in the window.

There is a message on the loud speaker. It is the security guard on the front desk who looks like Geoff Capes. Funnily enough, his name is actually Geoff and he seems to be quite a nice bloke.

"Please be advised that due to an error the fire alarm may go off in the next twenty minutes. Please ignore this alarm. I repeat, this is an error and so please ignore this alarm. Thank you."

I take another call. A man is not happy that he has not read the small print and he is not covered for what he thought he was covered for.

"Not a problem, sir," I say in a relaxed tone, "Please allow me look into the details for you."

"It may not be a problem for you," he barks, "but it is a problem for me."

I explain that I appreciate that it is a problem for him, but that it is not a problem for me to look into his concerns. It becomes clear again just how good I have become at talking bollocks and that, actually, I quite enjoy it. It is just a shame that I seem unable to put this into practice in the real world. I resolve his concerns as best as I can and the man thanks me.

"Not a problem," I repeat, and I end the call before he can shout at me.

Karen always seems to have more knowledge of my calls than she does of her own. I hear her guffawing from the other side of the desk.

"You do have a wicked way with words," she says.

There is another message from the loud speaker.

"Please be advised that if there is an actual fire we will be announcing this using the loud speaker system. I repeat, do not ignore the loud speaker announcement if there is a real fire."

Karen laughs louder than ever at this. "Oh Geoff, bless him," she sighs.

She looks around to make sure that nobody is listening and then whispers to me. I have never heard her whispering before. In fact, I was shopping in the Queens Arcade once and I'm sure I could hear her on her headset talking to a customer.

"Between me and you, Nick, I'd really like you to be my manager if you go for that job."

I feel my ears burn. I'd almost forgotten about the job that I was expected to go for, but it felt good to know that somebody appreciated me. I'd been far too pre-occupied thinking about the mess I'd made with Sara to worry about the promotion.

Karen leans forward even more.

"But I don't think I'd ever fully respect you as a person, Nick, if you let go what you had with that young Sara without putting up a fight," she whispers.

It was as if she was reading my mind.

Chapter Twenty Eight

People ask me what they should do about being in this business. I say learn the three R's: redundancy, rejection and rest – Victor Spinetti

Five months later…

"Course, there was a massive cast in the first movie," Den says, stubbing out his cigarette with the heel of his shoe. "It set the bar for all other casts. Of course, Stallone and Statham were the leads, but Jackie Chan had a decent part, and then there was Willis and Schwarzenegger, oh and not forgetting Cruise, of course."

"Cruise…?" I ask. I cannot for the life of me remember Tom Cruise being in the film. Surely I would have remembered? And he would only have accepted a lead role? "He weren't in it!" I protest.

"Course he was," Den says, nonchalantly. "Terry Crews! You know, the massively buff black guy from *Everybody Hates Chris.*"

"Terry Crews?" I ask, stifling a laugh. "I thought Glenn Webb played that part?"

It's Tuesday night, just before eight. We are standing outside the college cafeteria, on our ten minute break.

When Den told me he'd enrolled in an evening class, just two nights a week, I was proper chuffed for the guy. There were no two ways about it; it was a positive step. Then he asked whether I fancied enrolling, and I was like, no way I'm much too busy for that. I told Sara that he'd asked, she called me a selfish bastard, and the rest, as they say, is history. It is our fourth week on the course and, to be honest, I'm really getting into it. Not that I'm anywhere near as good as Den, though.

Den puts his hand to his mouth, drops his jaw, and yawns. The guy always looks knackered, like he's just got out of bed or something, and, to be fair, usually he just has. Over the last six weeks or so, though, he's tired because of the early shifts he's been putting in down the factory on the industrial estate. It's the first time that Den has done an honest day's work in years. He says the work is deadly dull, but that the lads are a good crack and can't really argue with the early finishes and the extra dough. I'm just glad he has a good reason to get up in the morning, rather than just drifting around, wasting away. We've even been able to discuss work together, which is a first, and in a way we're both 'newbies' as I'm only just settling into my role as team leader, with all the challenges that has to offer.

Den said that the biggest headache he had was telling his parents. He didn't think they'd be impressed that he was working in a factory, working with his hands. As it turns out, though, they were just happy that he was working at all. Their priorities had changed, just as I'd hoped they would. Den was sending a small wage back to Jamaica, and even Nan was now asking how he was getting on with his new job. Den's dad, apparently, had said something about being proud the way he'd coped after the death of his brother. Den couldn't even begin to describe how much that meant to him.

And he definitely has changed; you only need to look at him to see that. He still looks strong, but the bulk has gone, and now he looks lean, and perhaps because of this, he looks taller than ever I remember him. He is off the tablets and most of the exercise he gets now comes from working at the factory. He seems more talkative nowadays, like he has a genuine interest in what is going on outside his own little world.

"You're onto a good thing, there, mate," Den says. "Just make sure you don't let your best mate screw her this time, yeah?"

I laugh at this, possibly because it is closer to the bone than perhaps he realises. Den has met Sara loads of times now. The first time they'd met, though, was when we went for a quiet pint in town. I hadn't even made a link between him being my best mate and my best mate in London screwing my last missus. And then, as I was holding Sara's hand and we were just about to go into the pub, it suddenly clicked. The thought, though, came and went with the opening and closing of the pub door. I knew Den would never do that to me. And knowing I had a mate like that felt great.

And the two of them got on just brilliant, too.

"I can picture a couple of young Nick's running around in a couple of years," Den says, "so long as your Ellie Simmonds' are in good working order, of course."

"Ellie Simmonds?" I ask, genuinely perplexed.

"Little swimmers," Den says, matter-of-factly.

I laugh at this, but decide to move the conversation on.

"What about you, then, big man?" I ask. "Is there any possible romance blossoming?"

Den is the least likely person I know to have a blossoming romance, which is maybe why I ask the question.

He shakes his head, but there is something about the way he avoids eye contact. The guy definitely looks shifty. I punch him on the arm, probing for more information.

"Well, I've never said this to anyone before, but I've always imagined my ideal girl to be both Welsh and Jamaican, just like me..."

I laugh at this, because I'm pretty damn sure that such a girl doesn't even exist.

"Anyway, there aren't many of them around, granted," he continues. "But then four weeks ago, I saw her. She was possibly a couple of years younger than me, with all the assets you'd expect from a Caribbean kind of girl..." and he juts out his own arse as if to demonstrate. "And I tell you, this girl is just naturally pretty. Our eyes locked and she smiled at me, and I melted, you know? And then she spoke to one of her mates and she had the cutest Welsh accent I'd ever heard. I swear, brother, I thought that I'd died and gone to heaven, I tell you."

I still can't help but find this incredibly funny; my mate Den, the stud, being all coy and shy about some girl. I manage to restrain myself, though, and instead offer my hand, which he shakes, without fuss.

"All I need to do now is pluck up the courage to talk to

her," Den says. "I remember that time that you missed that sitter down the recreation centre, lost us the game, like. Well, I really respected you for that; for putting yourself in there where you were able to fall flat on your arse. I really need some of that kind of strength, mate."

I wish that he didn't have to talk quite so straight, but I know that there is a compliment in there, somewhere.

"You can do it, mate," I say. "Anyway, where did you see her?" I ask.

"Here," Den says. "She is doing some course. I see her every week and she always smiles."

A thought comes to me.

"Den, you know when we were in the tent down the beach and you asked me and Sam what we would have liked from life, well…"

"I only asked because I knew you two thought you were about to be brutally murdered and I'd get all sorts of revelations out of you…" Den interrupts, with a snigger.

"Yeah, well," I say, "I was just wondering what you would have said if we'd asked you, you know?"

Den stares at his shoe. I'm not sure whether he is thinking about his answer or thinking about how he can get out of answering.

"Well," he begins, "I'm a complex character, full of layers, like a double-decker chocolate bar, you know? I kind of think that the answer I'd give now wouldn't be the answer I'd have given then."

I can accept that. But I want more.

"So what would you have said then and what would you say now?" I prompt.

Den searches for the cigarettes from his pocket. "I think back then I would have asked for due respect from my parents. Right now, though, after everything that has happened, I just want to respect myself." He puts the pack of cigarettes back in his pocket; decides against lighting one. "Come on, big man," he says, "break must be nearly over."

This is our cue to go back to class. The stairs are steep and narrow. Den is bouncing on the balls of his feet. He takes two steps at a time.

It's as if he wants to make up for lost time, for not sticking with his gut and taking his Welsh A-Level all those years ago in school.

Chapter Twenty Nine

No-one knows why I'm called Jiffy, but if I tell you, I've got to kill you! – Jonathan Davies

My parents have just come home. Mum looks rosy-faced and Dad's hair is swept over his forehead, leaving half of his scalp bare. They are both noisier than usual.

"Where have you two trouble makers been?" Nan asks, from her usual seat next to the television.

She has been living with us since she went absent without leave. Somebody is always home and we are able to give her twenty-four hour care. Nan will either stay here forever or go into a home if her needs become too much. She seems blissfully unaware of this. Every single day she asks Mum when she is going home. And yet, in truth, she has settled in quite nicely. The woman is waited on hand and foot. For one thing, Nan is definitely enjoying the cooking. Her cheeks are plumper and the extra layers make her look younger, somehow.

"It's our 30th wedding anniversary, Joyce," my dad proudly tells her. "To celebrate, we have just been in a hot air balloon, and it was wonderful, wasn't it, love?"

Nan turns to me, her mouth wide open, gasping in shock. "Well, who would have thought? A hot air balloon, you say? Why ever would somebody want to do that, I ask you? Why ever would somebody want to do that?"

Actually, it was my idea. I'd learnt from Sara the importance of taking notice of other people, you know, like actually listening to what they say, and the like. Anyhow, one lazy Sunday afternoon my mum was in the garden when, lo and behold, a balloon floated past. Mum saw it and her eyes sparkled. "Oh, wouldn't you love to do that one day, Nick? How different would that be? Now, that would be living!"

I told her that it wasn't really my thing, but I dutifully reported the communication to my dad, and he purposefully set about researching on the internet. And by all accounts, the gift had been well-received.

"Up there in the sky, Mum, you have a real bird's eye view of everything, you know? You start to realise how small and insignificant your lives really are, and all your worries seem small and insignificant, too. It is almost spiritual, you know."

Nanny Joyce looks at me, her eyes wide and staring, as if to say 'who is this strange woman, and is she mad?'

Instead, though, she chuckles and says "who would have thought it, my own daughter in a hot air balloon!"

Nan is distracted by the weather coming on the TV. She doesn't leave the house much nowadays so I wouldn't have thought it would be too relevant. "Oh that Derek," she coos. "If I was fifty years younger, I tell you…."

Mother and daughter have been getting along swimmingly, considering they hadn't spoken to each other for twenty odd years. They say that part of the problem of a dispute is forgetting and forgiving. Luckily, Nan doesn't really seem to remember that they'd argued, so the forgetting part was already in the bag. She lives in the present. Her memories are mainly alive from fifty years ago, rather than fifty minutes.

Mum works tirelessly for Nan now, running around and checking that she is okay, almost every second of the day. However, amazingly, she looks so much more at ease. The life has gone back into her eyes. The bags have disappeared. I can only imagine that worrying about Nan took more out of her than actually being able to do something to help her.

It took me a week to pluck up the courage to even ask what had happened between them.

"Whatever do you mean, darling?" Mum asked.

"Well, you haven't talked for a long time, have you? And now it's as if you have never been apart."

"Ooh, I get you," she said, taking a sip of her tea.

And then she told me – just like that – without pausing or hesitating – and in great detail – absolutely everything. How Nan wasn't eighteen in the wedding photo; she was twenty-one. My mum was already three when the photo was taken.

The little gushing girl wasn't grumpy old Aunt Sally. It was Mum. Her dad couldn't cope with the pressure of being a teenage father. He'd been Nan's childhood sweetheart, her first love. He fled when Mum was just one. A year later, Nan met Albert, fell in love and they were quickly married. Albert took Mum on as his own daughter, and became the best father she could ever wish for.

"But Nan still brought you up? And you say you always knew that Albert wasn't your real dad? So when and why did you and Nan have a fall out?" I asked.

Mum looked a bit put out by this. She dipped a digestive in her tea and composed herself. "I was getting to that, Nick," she said. "It was when you were born, wasn't it?"

I should have known it would be my fault. It always is.

Mum seemed to sense my look and she patted my hand. "It wasn't your fault, silly!" she laughed. "It's just when you were born I made the biggest mistake of my life, something I've regretted to this day. I know what my thinking was, but it was still the wrong thing to do. I guess I wanted to preserve something of my real dad in you; that was all. But without doubt, you should have been named after the man who stood by me. You see, Nick, your middle name is from your real granddad, Harold."

I instantly thought back to that policeman in Cardiff demanding to know what my middle name was, and I think that he must have been trying to tell me something.

"Okay, but why did that cause your fall out, Mum?" I asked.

"Nan was livid, that's why. She loved Harold, but she hated him, too, for deserting her. She never visited his grave, but the more I heard about her confused state, I knew that's where she'd be. She loved Albert for being there for her, both when she was a single mother and for bringing me up. She never forgave me for doing that. We had the most terrible argument and we both said horrible, horrible things. She can be a strong, feisty woman when she wants to be, Nick, and I am just as bad. She felt that I'd betrayed her, darling."

I nodded my head. My mum was trembling. I could tell that she waited for my reaction. What I thought meant a lot to her, I could see that now. That's why she hadn't told me, all these years. I shrugged my shoulders. It really didn't mean anything to me. It was just a name. She was my mum and Nan is my nan, and the old-looking guy in the photo would always be my granddad.

Mum hugged me that night and sobbed on my shoulder.

"Well, we've had a whale of a time here, haven't we, err...." My Nan says now, pointing at me and searching for a name.

"Nick," I say, without pausing.

Nan chuckles. "Of course, Nick! How could I ever forget your name dear?" she asks.

She forgets it all the time, to be honest, but I'm used to it now.

The doorbell rings and in bounds Den. He marches over to Nan and gives her a kiss on the cheek.

"Ahh, Den, how are you love? And how is your mother?"

"She is good, Nanny Joyce," Den says.

I can't remember the last time Nan saw Den but they are like best mates.

He calls out to my mother. "There is a concert tonight for Jason Thomas, you know the young lad who got run over by a tractor. It's a sell out, you know. I was thinking something like that might be a good idea for Patrick?"

Mum is in the kitchen, washing the dishes. She is so on the go nowadays that even some of my dad's jobs have been taken away from him. He is fine with that, he just paints more. Both Mum and Nan say it's a wonderful idea, even though I'm sure Nan doesn't have a clue who this Patrick they're talking about is.

"Anyway, Mrs Evans, I was just going to wish Nick here the best for his London trip. Sara is a really nice girl, don't you think?"

"Yes," my Mum shouts back from the kitchen. "We really like her. Charles and I are so proud that Nick has finally met a nice girl, not like that last girlfriend, Katie, the brazen hussy..."

I think all three of us in the lounge look at each other and raise our eyebrows. How things have changed.

Chapter Thirty

When it comes to one great score
To mark against your name
He'll not ask how you played the game
But…whether you beat England – Max Boyce

London

When Sara told me she'd never been to London before, I kind of assumed she was pulling my leg. The thing is; she's good at that. She does it all the time. And so I just went along with the little charade, just for a while, you know, until she got bored of it. But she kept up with her story, telling me how she should have gone with the Girl Guides when she was nine but she got chickenpox and stayed in bed all weekend instead. And then how, when she was twenty, she was all booked to go on a hen do but the groom got caught in a compromising position with the chief bridesmaid, and so that weekend was called off, too. Damn that chief bridesmaid, Sara said. It was fate, she continued. She was never destined to go to London Town. It was just never meant to be. Sara continued in this vein for such a long time I figured that, just this once, she wasn't pulling my leg after all.

"You're fucking with me?" I eventually asked, borrowing one of her prized sayings.

Sara pulled on my ears, puckered her lips, and gave me a kiss. "Oh, babe, would I ever fuck with you?' she asked, feigning horror and hurt, like butter wouldn't melt in her mouth.

We took the train to Paddington from Cardiff Central straight after work last night, hurriedly dropped our bags off at our hotel in Bayswater and then headed straight out for something to eat and drink. In between mouthfuls of fine food, expensive wine and fast, breathless chatter, Sara gazed open-eyed at the street outside. Her blue eyes flickered with excitement. Sara was amazed by the constant, endless stream of cars, buses and pedestrians that passed.

"It's just so happening, don't you think, Nick?" she asked, fork dangling precariously from her lips.

I wasn't expecting all this enthusiasm and goodwill from Sara. I was anticipating quite the opposite, in fact. I thought she'd berate all the money, moan about the pretentiousness of it all, ask what all the fuss was about, and so-on-and-so-on.

And yet, she's been the total opposite.

Today we've played at being tourists. We sat on the top floor of the double-decker bus as we crossed Tower Bridge. Sara pointed at the boats in the Thames and screamed when she spotted the wheel further down the river. She marveled at the history and the architecture and beauty that seemed to be everywhere she looked. My girlfriend seemed to look at things with completely different eyes than I did when I lived here.

And now, exiting the underground at Oxford Circus, the light has drawn in and there is a definite chill in the air. Enthusiasm must be infectious, because the two of us are feverish with excitement. We dodge in and out of the flow of pedestrians, holding hands where we can. The air is filled with an aroma of roasting chestnuts. We exchange breathless, occasional chatter.

"The thing is, Nicholas..." Sara begins, and I just know by the use of Nicholas rather than Nick or babe or darling or any other of the affectionate pet names she uses for me, that I'm in for a lecture, "...all the time I've known you, you've been putting London down, you know?"

"I have?"

"Of course you have, Nicholas," Sara exclaims. "But you know what I'm thinking, now? I think it was the way you were in London that was the problem, and not London itself, you know what I mean?"

I squeeze her hand. It is difficult to engage in conversation when you're concentrating on not bumping into an avalanche of people. I guess Sara can manage it because she's a lady and she can multi-task.

"But now you're really able to enjoy it for what it is, aren't you, darling? And I guess that having a beautiful lady by your side to enjoy it with makes it a bit easier, no?" She giggles. "You've definitely changed, though, Nick, from the guy I first met. And it's for the good, I think. In the words of Louis Walsh, 'you've been on a journey, Nick!'"

I've been thinking much the same myself, to be honest. It's fair to say that when I was in London, I felt I'd proved something by getting out of Bridgend, by just being a player in the big city. And so, when I returned home with my tail between my legs, I felt I had to big up the reasons for coming back. I was playing the two places against each other, and now I know there was no need to, not really. Both London and Bridged have a place in my heart, to be fair, although having said that, deep down, I now know that Bridgend is where I feel most at home.

"I have no idea what you're talking about, Sara," I say flatly, but she knows I'm smiling.

Enrolling on the evening degree course in psychology was the best decision she's ever made. Now she has a goal and an objective that was missing before. Not to mention that the subject seems absolutely made for her.

We're a bit lost now, though. The theatre is further west, I know that, so we've definitely been heading in the right general direction, but the turnoff I've been looking for has gone missing. I make a decision. We turn down a side street, one that feels familiar.

It's a narrow little road, and it's sheltered from the drizzling rain by the tall, grey buildings on both sides. It's not a straight path, either, so I can't see where it leads to. I'm sensing that my instinct has failed me. It's too quiet to lead towards the theatre. I check my watch. It's not a big problem. We still have plenty of time.

I'm about to turn round when I notice a commotion up ahead. I'd already spotted the man sat on the floor, legs crossed, tattered jeans resting on a colorless, dirty sleeping bag. The man looks old, but that might be because of his straggly unkempt beard and the ingrained dirt on his face. I'd seen the two men leaning over and talking to him, all friendly, and I'd suspected that maybe they were a little too friendly, like they were making fun. I'm right. One of the men picks up the bucket full of coins from the floor and dangles it in the man's face, teasing him.

And that's when the commotion really begins. Three women appear from around the corner, high heels clicking against the concrete floor, handbags swinging. They are glamorous, with long full hair, frilly dresses and sparkling earrings. I take another look. No, they are not women after all. They are men, dressed in drag. They look like artists, like professional performers. And in their own individual way, they look sensational.

There are a few threats. One of the women lunges forward and grabs hold of the plastic bucket with both hands. The men aren't frightened, though. They start laughing, mockingly. They don't see tall, masculine men dressed up as drag artists. They see three women; and three easy targets at that. I know it's going to get nasty, and I roll up the sleeves on my coat and clench my fist. I really, really hope that it *doesn't* get nasty, though.

The first man in drag takes a step back and throws a perfect left hook flush against the man's jaw. He staggers back. I'm sure that if it wasn't for the support of the wall, he'd have fallen flat on his ass. He puts his hand on his chin, disbelievingly looks at his mate, throws the bucket to the floor, and they both run off

The three women find all of this hilarious. There are a few high fives. The one with the wicked left hook perches down and gives the bucket to the homeless man. The man has a big goofy smile on his face now, and rocks his head back and forth.

The women continue walking down the street towards us, hips swiveling, bravado intact. The heroine chatters breathlessly. The woman that he is portraying is what most people would describe as conventionally beautiful, with high cheekbones, smooth skin and long, fluttering lashes. He seems completely and utterly at home in his attire, I can tell. He cares not what others think. Our eyes meet as he passes, and there is a brief moment of hesitation before he smiles and continues walking, along the narrow path and out into the madness of the main street. I hear Sara exchange polite hellos with the other two artists.

My left foot moves one way and my right moves the other, just like they did all those years ago in the gymnasium, and I end up moving nowhere at all. Sara thinks that I'm contemplating which direction we should go. I pull out my phone, and she asks how I am, what I am doing. I lightly shrug her off and dial a number. I'm breathing heavily now. The phone is ringing. I hear a friendly, bubbly voice.

"Sam's alive," I say.

Lightning Source UK Ltd.
Milton Keynes UK
UKOW04f2008180913

217477UK00001B/12/P

9 781909 220553